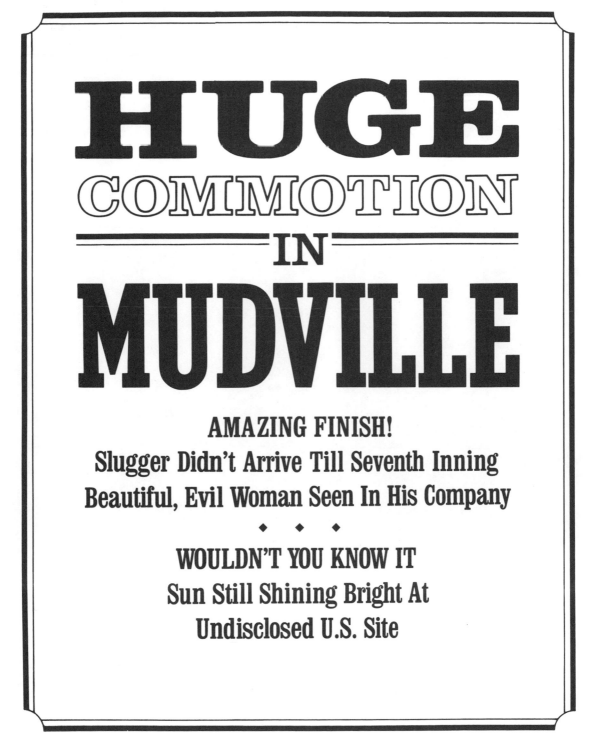

CASEY
◄ ON THE ►
LOOSE

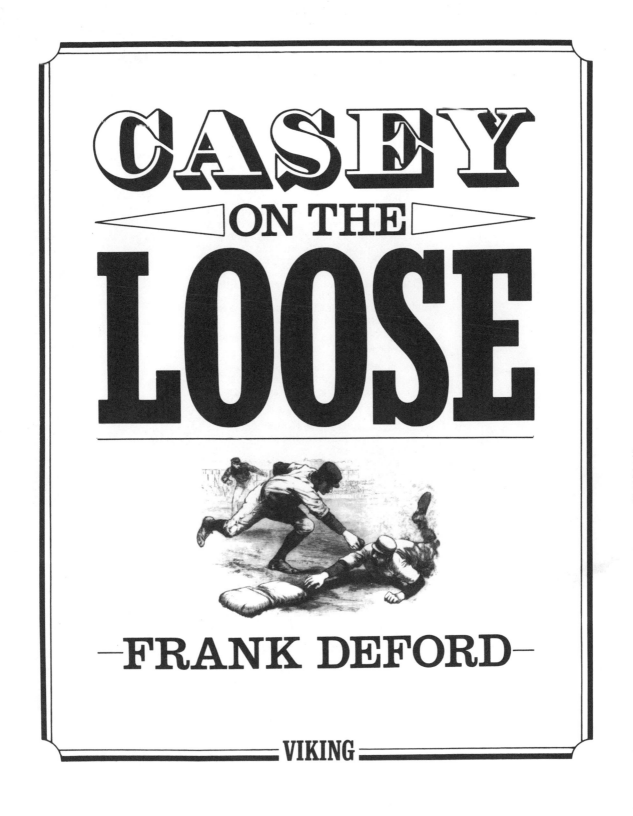

— FRANK DEFORD —

VIKING

VIKING
Published by the Penguin Group
Viking Penguin, a division of Penguin Books USA Inc.,
40 West 23rd Street, New York, New York 10010, U.S.A.
Penguin Books Ltd, 27 Wrights Lane,
London W8 5TZ, England
Penguin Books Australia Ltd, Ringwood,
Victoria, Australia
Penguin Books Canada Ltd, 2801 John Street,
Markham, Ontario, Canada L3R 1B4
Penguin Books (N.Z.) Ltd, 182–190 Wairau Road,
Auckland 10, New Zealand

Penguin Books Ltd, Registered Offices:
Harmondsworth, Middlesex, England

First pubished in 1989 by Viking Penguin,
a division of Penguin Books USA Inc.
Published simultaneously in Canada

1 3 5 7 9 10 8 6 4 2

Copyright © Frank Deford, 1989
All rights reserved

This book is based on Mr. Deford's "Casey at the Bat,"
which appeared in *Sports Illustrated*. © 1988 Time Inc.

LIBRARY OF CONGRESS CATALOGING IN PUBLICATION DATA
Deford, Frank.
Casey on the loose.
I. Title.
PS3554.E37C37   1989   813′.54   88-40524
ISBN 0-670-82780-0

Printed in the United States of America
Set in Ionic No. 5
Designed by Michael Ian Kaye
Photographs by Abe Seltzer

It is now a quarter of a century since the game of base ball became popularized as the game of games of American youth; and within that period it has so extended itself in its sphere of operations that it is now the permanently established national field game of America. Not even the great war of the rebellion could check its progress to any great extent; in fact, in one way— through the national army—it led to its being planted in a Southern clime, and now base ball can be said to "know no North, no South, no East, no West."

—Introduction,
*Spalding's Official
Base Ball Guide,*
1888

A List of the Chapters in this Tale Are Here Subjoined

EVEN THE PEOPLE
WHO WRITE ABOUT BASEBALL
HAVE A TEAM THEY GROW UP WITH AND
ALWAYS CHEER FOR, JUST LIKE NORMAL FANS DO. SO,
THIS ISN'T FOR THE WRITER IN ME, BUT FOR THE
FAN . . . AND IT IS FOR BROOKS
AND JIM, F. ROBBY AND
BOOG AND EARL.

CASEY AT THE BAT

A Ballad of the Republic

By

Ernest L. Thayer

◆ ◆ ◆

THE OUTLOOK wasn't brilliant for the Mudville nine that day; ◆ The score stood four to two with but one inning more to play. ◆ And then when Cooney died at first, and Barrows did the same, ◆ A sickly silence fell upon the patrons of the game.

A STRAGGLING few got up to go in deep despair. The rest ◆ Clung to that hope which springs eternal in the human breast; ◆ They thought if only Casey could but get a whack at that— ◆ We'd put up even money now with Casey at the bat.

BUT FLYNN preceded Casey, as did also Jimmy Blake, ◆ And the former was a lulu and the latter was a cake; ◆ So upon the stricken multitude grim melancholy sat, ◆ For there seemed but little chance of Casey's getting to the bat. ◆

BUT FLYNN let drive a single, to the wonderment of all, ◆ And Blake, the much despis-ed, tore the cover off the ball; ◆ And when the dust had lifted, and the men saw what had occurred, ◆ There was Jimmy safe at second and Flynn a-hugging third. ◆

THEN FROM 5,000 throats and more there rose a lusty yell; ◆ It rumbled through the valley, it rattled in the dell; ◆ It knocked upon the moun-tain and recoiled upon the flat, ◆ For Casey, mighty Casey, was advancing to the bat. ◆

THERE WAS ease in Casey's manner as he stepped into his place; ◆ There was pride in Casey's bearing and a smile on Casey's face. ◆ And when, responding to the cheers, he lightly doffed his hat, ◆ No stranger in the crowd could doubt 'twas Casey at the bat. ◆

TEN THOUSAND eyes were on him as he rubbed his hands with dirt; ◆ Five thousand tongues applauded when he wiped them on his shirt. ◆ Then while the writhing pitcher ground the ball into his hip, ◆ Defiance gleamed in Casey's eye, a sneer curled Casey's lip. ◆

AND NOW the leather-covered sphere came hurtling through the air, ◆ And Casey stood a-watching it in haughty grandeur there. ◆ Close by the sturdy batsman the ball unheeded sped—, ◆ "That ain't my style," said Casey. "Strike one," the umpire said. ◆

FROM THE benches, black with people, there went up a muffled roar, ◆ Like the beating of the storm-waves on a stern and distant shore. ◆ "Kill him! Kill the umpire!" shouted some one on the stand; ◆ And it's likely they'd have killed him had not Casey raised his hand. ◆

WITH A SMILE of Christian charity great Casey's visage shone; ◆ He stilled the rising tumult; he bade the game go on; ◆ He signaled to the pitcher, and once more the spheroid flew; ◆ But Casey still ignored it, and the umpire said, "Strike two." ◆

"FRAUD!" CRIED the maddened thousands, and echo answered fraud; ◆ But one scornful look from Casey, and the audience was awed. ◆ They saw his face grow stern and cold, they saw his muscles strain, ◆ And they knew that Casey wouldn't let that ball go by again. ◆

THE SNEER is gone from Casey's lip, his teeth are clenched in hate; ◆ He pounds with cruel violence his bat upon the plate. ◆ And now the pitcher holds the ball, and now he lets it go, ◆ And now the air is shattered by the force of Casey's blow. ◆

OH, SOMEWHERE in this favored land the sun is shining bright; ◆ The band is playing somewhere, and somewhere hearts are light, ◆ And somewhere men are laughing, and somewhere children shout; ◆ But there is no joy in Mudville—mighty Casey has struck out. ◆

And
so, if ever you
loved baseball, or if
ever you had a hero, surely
you would like to know more about
Casey, know who his friends were (and
who his enemies were), know what he was
doing back there a century ago when Ernest
Thayer wrote his "Ballad of the Republic"
—and know what ever happened to
mighty Casey after he struck out
in the bottom of the ninth,
Saturday, June 2, 1888.
Wouldn't you?
And so . . .

To save money the team owner, grumpy old Cyrus Weatherly (in top hat), only included the starting nine of the Mudville team in this official photograph taken on May 16, 1888, two weeks before the game. Top row, left to right: Hughie Barrows, 3b; William O. Flaherty, mgr; John Arthur Cooney, c; Barry O'Connor, p. Third row: Amos (Yesterday) Phillips, cf; Weatherly himself; Henry (Dandy Dutch) Bismarck, 1b. Second row: Timothy F. X. Casey, rf; Johnny Flynn, 2b. First row: Ezekial (Salty) Phizer, lf; Jimmy Blake, ss.

many men who have succeeded in his profession—Fox was an editor—his strength lay in the deployment of better men's talents. About his throat, open side down, he wore a horseshoe pin of gold, studded with diamonds.

Fox settled in his seat and turned to the newspapers. General Sheridan—old Fightin' Phil of the Federal cavalry—was fading fast, "tided over only by oxygen and electricity." The Republicans were assembled in Chicago, seeking to find the nominee best able to run against the incumbent Democrat, Grover Cleveland. The President's own party would itself convene Saturday in St. Louis, but the papers, their news priorities ever straight, were much more interested in what the President's beautiful child wife, his former ward, the twenty-three-year-old Frances Folsom, had worn yesterday at Decoration Day ceremonies.

Fox turned to the inside pages. The New Hampshire legislature had turned down the right of females to vote. Uh-huh. Several fool immigrants who didn't know how to swim had, predictably, died of drowning on the holiday. Won't these people ever learn? Business remained at sixes and sevens waiting to see if the Republicans might get into the White House and raise tariffs. A circus train had been derailed in Springfield, Massachusetts, and a boa constrictor was on the loose. Students attending the International YMCA Training School were leading the hunt for the killer snake. Hmmm. And the classifieds: teamsters were needed, street sweepers, varnishers, wet nurses, able-bodied hands to work a fishing boat for $3.50 a day "till the snow flies."

1

GOING AFTE
THE CHAMPI

The porters scram
Richard Fox's b
rived at Grand (
that bright Thursday
a century ago, May 3
ton" was all Fox said, and the luc
his valise rushed ahead to the Pu
his leisure, pausing to buy a sele
and a bright boutonniere. He wa
a mustache too bushy for his li
half, and cold, hooded eyes. Bu
pect of his animal namesake,

Another page or two riffled, and Fox found himself in the sports section. Now he was home.

The sports section in the 'eighties—the eighteen-eighties—had suddenly become a popular force. For the cranks—what baseball fans were so aptly known as then—reporters traveled with the home teams, supplying firsthand coverage from distant ports of call, and the major-league box scores were telegraphed from all over. There was the venerable National League—most often, just: The League—and the upstart American Association. The Association was enough. Plus even line scores of the burgeoning minor leagues. If Fox had looked closely, for example, he would have seen the scores from the Bay State League, which included this holiday doubleheader result: Mudville 15, 7–Lynn 5, 2.

There was also plenty of boxing news for the fancy (as the pugilistic world preferred to style itself), as well as other sports for every taste: horse racing, horse shows, crew, tennis, golf, lacrosse, cricket and many other activities to amuse more and more of these citified Americans. No one single person, either, was more responsible for this boom—or, even more so, its profit—than Richard Fox, who had made his magazine, *The National Police Gazette,* a successful publication and an American barbershop institution largely because of sport.

Then one item down near the bottom of the *Tribune*'s sports page caught Fox's eye: CHAMPION RETURNS FROM EUROPE. John L. Sullivan, the brief report said, had arrived back in Boston and would be engaging in some exhibitions on stage. "Champion," Fox muttered, crumpling up the paper. "Just a fat Mick lout." John L. Sullivan was Richard Fox's one *bête noire,* for he couldn't control Sullivan. Indeed, all Fox did to contest the Boston Strong Boy only served to enhance his reputation. Fox had put up Paddy Ryan, the very specimen of a man, to fight Sullivan in '82 in Mississippi City, Mississippi, and Sullivan put Ryan down nine times before the poor challenger's handlers threw in the sponge after only ten minutes and thirty seconds. Not only that, but the victory utterly established Sullivan as the first truly great American athletic hero . . . world athletic hero.

Still, Sullivan showed no gratitude. He wouldn't do Fox's bidding, wouldn't defend his title again. Instead, he went about making a tarnished fortune fighting exhibitions—"My name is John L. Sullivan, and I can beat any sonuvabitch in the house"—and eat everything in the house too, gulping bourbon from beer steins and whoring away what was left of his free time. Frustrated, Fox made up a magnificent *Police Gazette* "championship" belt for the pretender, Jake Kilrain. So . . . so, last August the 7th of '87, at the Boston Theatre itself, the whole damn city of Boston gave Sullivan an even grander bejeweled belt—397 diamonds, worth $10,000—and The Great John L. grew greater still.

Nothing Fox wrote, nothing he said, nothing he schemed, made a dent in his nemesis. So, this morning, when the train to Boston pulled out of Grand Central, generously donating soot to New York, it was carrying the mountain to Mohammed. This time, at last, Fox was going to goad the champion in person, and, somehow, force him to defend his title again ... for the greater good of mankind, America and *Police Gazette* newsstand sales. "The Great John L.," Fox muttered. "My great arse."

THE COMPANY CASEY KEEPS

About the time Fox's Pullman passed through Bridgeport, up in Boston, in the South End, Chester Drinkwater escorted a handsome young couple into the amazing Cyclorama on Tremont Street. Their names were Florence Maureen Cleary and Timothy F. X. Casey, and their eyes grew as wide as their mouths, for there before them, all around them, in a circular vista, four hundred feet in circumference, fifty feet high, even bigger than most any cathedral, there was the entire Battle of Gettysburg: Little Round Top, Culp's Hill, The Peach Orchard . . . Pickett's Charge! Casey didn't have to have any of it explained to him, either. He might not have been born till '67, but his father had fought in the War, wearing blue, and his mother's favorite brother had died at Antietam, all bloody gray. Casey knew his War. Casey knew his America.

And was America a-boomin' now! The West filling, the cities bursting their seams, begging for immigrants from anywhere to fill the factories, with trolleys (some actually electric!) carrying the middle classes out into those new places called suburbs. Industry. Commerce. Jobs. Science! Inventions! Dreams!! America!! The streets were not only jammed, but, above them, everywhere there were these *wires* now. Telegraph lines, telephone lines, electric lines! Yet, figure it out: America in '88 was still closer to Gettysburg than to the Ardennes, closer to Jeb Stuart than to Sergeant York, closer to Abraham Lincoln than to, uh, Babe Ruth. The country was like a teen-age boy growing out of control, his voice and his legs going this way and that at all the wrong times.

Flossie Cleary had, of course, heard tell about Gettysburg, but she hadn't got off the boat from Cork until '84, and she was overwhelmed more by the scope of the Cyclorama than by the fearful scenes it depicted. So Casey took it upon himself to fill her in. Here is where the battle was first joined. Here is where Lee put his artillery. Meade's headquarters were over this way, and now when Longstreet moved on Cemetery Ridge, down— Uh oh. Casey's hand went out, and it grazed against Flossie's bosom. Grazed. Lingered. And then it was gone, and Casey was telling Flossie about the cavalry, but she didn't hear a word. How many times had she whispered to Father O'Reilly in the confessional that she had sinned, for hoping Casey just might touch her . . . and now he had . . . and as Father O'Reilly knew so well by now, Flossie didn't trust herself at all with Casey, not even during the day, and here they would be alone tonight. Chaperoned by Mr. Chester Drinkwater and his spinster sister Maud, of course, but alone all the same, at beautiful, alluring Nantasket Beach. Different rooms in the hotel. Of course. Different floors. Of course. Of course, but still. There was so much about this that left Flossie uneasy; in fact, it was easy to be uneasy about Timothy; Chester Drinkwater was harder still to accept, on any terms.

"Ah, Timothy, but exactly who might be this Mr. Drinkwater, and why would he be doing these lovely things for you?" Flossie had asked when Casey first told her that he had this benefactor, this high-class sporting man, this rich crank, who wanted to take them to Nantasket, in his own surrey, in his own sloop across Hingham Bay, put them up there at the finest hotel, take them to the finest dinner and the finest show.

"Flossie, would you be lookin' a gift horse in the mouth?" Casey replied, and a bit testily. "Mr. Chester Drinkwater is not only a sporting man, but one of the most successful businessmen in Boston. Why, they call him The Trolley King! Not only does he own several trolley lines, but he is the man who owns Norumbega Amusement Park in Newton."

Flossie gasped. "Are you telling me that this gentleman himself owns Norumbega?" Casey just smiled smugly, nodding even before she finished asking. "Timothy Casey, you wouldn't be pulling the long bow on me now, would you?"

"Mr. Drinkwater himself owns Norumbega itself," Casey said, and while Flossie fanned herself at this revelation—Norumbega was surely a marvel of our time—still, something stayed under her fair skin. Something troubled her.

On the occasion of this exchange Flossie and Casey had been alone on the magnificent veranda at the stylish house with the mansard roof in the finest section of Mudville, where Flossie was employed as a downstairs maid by Mr. and Mrs. Alfred L. Evans Jr. But she turned away from Casey, fretting, looking out to the gazebo. Things were suspicious and moving altogether too fast. Never mind Chester Drinkwater. It had been quite enough, her going ahead and falling head-over-heels in love with a ballist.

Now, only a very few years ago, baseball was pretty respectable. It was usually thought of as town ball, because the local team was made up, simply enough, by the leading young citizens of the community. But the game was too popular for its own good, and, almost overnight, it had been professionalized by transients: town ball to base-ball to baseball. Why, up until just the very last year, 1887, a batter could ask the pitcher to throw the ball where he wanted it, but that sort of politeness was fast disappearing. Already, in most quarters, baseball players were being written off as riff-raff, which was fair enough, because most of them were. Ballplayers in 1888 generally drank too much, smoked and spit, gambled and separated young ladies from their virtue whenever they chanced to bump into any female of even passing chastity. Mostly, ballists consorted with other lowlifes, such as actors, dance hall girls, boodlers, flimflammers, second-story types, chippies, tarts and cracksmen.

In the off-season a great many players even worked on stage or with a circus. Casey had joined the Mudville nine late in the '87 season, and had first met Flossie then, but he'd gone away soon enough, traveling with Barnum & Bailey. Mostly he labored as a roustabout for the sideshow, although he and another strong young man were dressed in leopard skins at show time and paid another four bits a day to come up on stage and try to (unsuccessfully) hoist the fat lady.

Casey frightened Flossie some, because even though she loved him, he remained a bit mysterious. While Flossie was the one who had just barely come to America, Casey seemed more alone and certainly more independent. She brought that up one time—sort of, kind of brought it up. "It's funny about America, you'll see," Casey replied. "It's a very exuberant place, but the ones just got here tend to be the ones feel they have to make the most commotion. I'd rather you just watch my smoke"—and he winked.

Then, too, Casey *was* alone. His mother had died after giving him birth, and it was only a few years after that when his father was killed in an accident on the docks. That was in Baltimore, where Casey was born and raised. His only sibling was his left-handed twin sister, Kate (older by eight minutes), but she left the orphan asylum as soon as she could and married into a German family, so Casey'd all but lost touch with her, except maybe when the circus came through Baltimore.

"It's just this baseball craze, Flossie," Casey said, moving over to stand by her on the veranda. "Americans just think it's a humdinger. Not just Chester Drinkwater. Not just in Mudville. There's new teams and whole new leagues all over the Republic. Stadiums you wouldn't believe. Why, I hear tell that the South End Grounds—"

"In Boston."

"Yeah, where the Beaneaters play. The pharaohs would trade their old pyramids for that. And the cranks—the way they fuss about us players. Why, did you know what when the Beaneaters won the championship, somebody that Jim Galvin didn't even—"

"Jim who?"

"Jim Galvin, the team's best wheelman. Some crank just sent him a *forty*-five-dollar overcoat. Just a present. From a total stranger." Flossie swooned. "And then, this year, the Beaneaters paid ten thousand dollars to the Chicagos just to obtain the services of King Kelly for Boston."

Flossie gasped, which was better than swooning, because it allowed her to reach out naturally and touch Casey's hand. Ten thousand dollars was more money than she expected to see in her lifetime. But she could see that something surely was happening in the 'eighties.

For baseball was developing as a kind of adhesive that held together the evolving modern city and all its diverse types. Football was another newfangled game, but it was only for college boys trying to show that they could still be as tough in their spare time as the working people had to be for a living. Baseball was for the people—and especially in the new industrial metropolises. The South, which was still primarily rural, even had to import most of its ballists when the minor leagues began to take hold down there. But wherever some middling city aspired to the big time, it was being said that it needed three things: trolley lines, an opera house and a baseball team.

"What can I do, Flossie?" Casey asked. "I just found out I could hit a horsehide, and people love me for it."

IN WHICH
MRS. EVANS
ATTENDS A GAME

Mudville had gone bonkers over its local nine that spring of '88, and it was almost entirely due to Casey. Soon his name was everywhere, even in the best of circles. Still, Mr. and Mrs. Alfred L. Evans Jr., being protective and paternal when it came to their domestics, didn't want their Flossie having anything to do with a ballist. Certainly they would not allow a ballist to come round to their fine house with the mansard roof on Elm Street.

But the best way to obtain such a grand house in America was to be a banker, and Mr. Evans was—second vice-

president of The First Farmers and Mechanics Bank of Mudville. And if you are a banker you can take the afternoon off
when you feel like it, and one day Mr. Evans did, and went
out to the ballyard and saw Mudville take on Framingham.
And what a swell game for the home team! Not only did
Mudville's best pitcher, Barry O'Connor, throw a Chicago—
which is what a shutout was known as in those days—but
Casey hit two triplets and a two-bagger and enthralled the
crowd throughout. Mudville 8–Framingham 0.

Mr. Evans, who had played some third base for the old
Mudville town team a few years before (and who could larrup
the sphere pretty good, if he did occasionally still say so
himself), went home then and called Flossie into the parlor
and advised her that, under the proper conditions, *well chaperoned, of course*—"Yes sir, of course"—it would be appro-
priate for her to see this young Mr. Casey . . . if Mrs. Evans
approved, of course.

"Yes sir, of course."

Then Mr. Evans kept Flossie there for a few more minutes
and told her all about the time he'd knocked the cover off
the ball in the ninth against Haverhill, drove in two runs and
won the match for Mudville.

As for Casey, this glorious spring of '88, he'd walloped a
homer on Opening Day and kept up the tattoo all spring.
Why, not a single pitcher had yet managed to strike him out.
The ball didn't have much bounce in it back then, and the
wheelman was delivering from only fifty feet away, but Casey
had such power that soon enough the sports pages had

Baseball was developing
as a kind of adhesive that held
together the evolving modern city
and all its diverse types

named him: Mighty Casey. He was hitting .386, too, and making circus catches in the outfield.

Grumpy old Cyrus Weatherly, the town miser, who owned the team and the Mudville Grounds as well, was particularly delighted to see that, soon enough, a few respectable women started coming out to the games, and, and awhile, even some of the town's elite, ladies and gentlemen of the first order, began easing over to the East Side to catch the games. On Mr. Evans's urging, Mrs. Evans invited Flossie to accompany her to the Grounds one fine Wednesday afternoon when the Brockton nine was in town.

The two ladies bought the best seats, in the fourth row, down the first-base line, and while Flossie was sure Casey had spotted her, they avoided each other's eyes. But then, just before Mudville came up in the seventh, Flossie stood up to straighten her dress, and Casey was leading off, and when he stepped toward the plate, he couldn't help but see her, and he nodded to her and smiled from under his white cap with the maroon bill, and then, after she blushed, straightaway Casey fell into the pitcher's first delivery, put the lash to it and drove it over the leftfield fence, putting Mudville ahead 4–3. Flossie was even more mortified when Casey crossed the plate and tipped his hat to her. The whole crowd looked at Flossie and cheered louder still.

Mrs. Evans glanced down at her scorecard. It would be several more decades before players would be assigned numbers on their uniforms, but at least they were identified in the scorecard. "Timothy F. X. Casey, Baltimore, 4/17/67,"

Mrs. Evans read. And then, out loud: "Six feet, one hundred and seventy-five. Rightfield."

"Yes ma'm."

"What does the F.X. stand for?"

"Francis Xavier," Flossie replied. "Of course, and that would be the only thing I've ever heard F.X. to stand for."

"Well, he is an awfully fine-looking lad," Mrs. Evans went on, examining Casey, over on the bench.

"Yes'm, some would say," Flossie ventured at last, brimming with crimson, trying to pretend as if she were concentrating on Amos "Yesterday" Phillips, the next Mudville batsman.

"Do you know much about this Mr. Casey, Flossie? Ballists are not always the best sort for a proper young lady such as yourself to associate with."

"Oh, yes'm, I do know that. But Timothy's such a nice lad, I promise you."

"Yes, but what does he promise *you?*" Flossie lowered her head. The count went full on Phillips. "I don't have to remind you about the sad business of Bridget and Clancy O'Toole." No, most assuredly Flossie did not have to be reminded of that. Bridget Corcoran was the upstairs maid and O'Toole the ice-wagon boy; he had taken full advantage of her.

Yesterday Phillips blooped a single to center.

"Where did you meet Mr. Casey?" Mrs. Evans went on.

"Oh, he just saw me putting out the wash one day last September shortly after he joined the nine, he did, and he strolled over and introduced himself, and he told me I had a pleasing aspect, and could he see me again?"

"And what did you say?"

"Why, Mrs. Evans, of course now, I said No. And very emphatically I did."

"Well good, Florence."

"But then I saw him one time at Mass, and on that occasion I allowed him to address me briefly."

"He wasn't fresh, was he?"

"Oh, no'm. Not a'tall. And he didn't even tell me he was such a fine ballist. Here the whole town was taking a shine to him, and I didn't have the foggiest, I didn't, until Bandy, the butcher boy, told me." Dandy Dutch Bismarck strode to the plate. "And then, when first I came to the Grounds here one afternoon, me day off, o'course, with Colleen, and I saw Timothy at the bat, saw the defiance in his eye and a sneer curling his lip—why, I couldn't believe that it was the same fellow I lo—" Flossie stopped. Uh oh. But it was too late.

"That you *loved?*" Mrs. Evans said. But sweetly—just-us-girls. Not nosy.

Flossie ducked her head and didn't even look up when the crowd oohed and ahhed as Dandy Dutch lifted a long fly to center.

"Yes'm. You see now, so many times I've seen such a smile of Christian charity shining on Timothy's visage."

"I'm sure, Flossie," Mrs. Evans said, patting her knee. "And I wholeheartedly agree with Mr. Evans that we should get a look at this young man."

"Oh thank you," Flossie cried out, and she was still beaming, even as she blushed, when Casey left the Grounds after the game. Mudville had stayed on top after Casey put them ahead with his homer in the seventh, and there was a big crowd waiting for the home team when it came out. The players were all in their uniforms, going back to their board-inghouses to change. They had to purchase their own uniforms in those days and pay for their own cleaning too, which is why the uniforms were rarely new and almost always dirty. Still, notwithstanding the players' vocational aroma, the cranks pressed upon them. Casey and the others could move along fairly well, though, because as yet nobody had thought of asking athletes for specimens of their signatures. None-theless, one rather ascetic, beetle-browed young man was too timid to bull his way to Casey, much as it was obvious that Casey was the one he had come to see.

At that next instant, then, just as the shy fellow did start to close on Casey, Casey spotted Flossie, and he called out her name and burst through the crowd to reach her.

Lest Casey be so indecorous as to touch her, Flossie quickly said, "Timothy, if you please, this is Mrs. Evans, my mistress, and she would like it very much indeed if you would come over and have some lemonade and cake with us."

Luckily, Casey got hold of himself, whipped off his Mudville cap, and told Mrs. Evans that he would be only too delighted. "I'll just have to change my togs first, ma'm," he said.

"Fine," Mrs. Evans replied, "but do bring your uniform with you, and we'll put it out with the family wash."

"Oh, yes ma'm, yes indeed," Casey said, and then he ran off, weaving through the crowd with such nimble agility that the ascetic-looking young man lost him again in the crunch.

4

TWO VISITORS TO THE HOUSE ON ELM STREET

Casey came by the Evanses' after a bit, dressed in his new suit, which was in a "whiskey" shade (all the rage for gentlemen that spring). Mr. Evans was home from the bank by now, and he and Mrs. Evans and the two young people had quite a gay old time of it. Casey made a fine impression indeed.

But then there was a rap on the door, and who should it be but the shy fellow who had been out at the Grounds. He explained that he had been directed here from Casey's boardinghouse, and so Mr. Evans steered him out to the veranda, where everyone was forgathered. "Mr. Casey," the young gentleman began, "my name is Jim Naismith, and I'm down from the Dominion of Canada. I'm a Christian, and I believe that His word can also be spread in athletics. I'm planning to become what they call a teacher of physical education over at the International YMCA Training School in Springfield."

"How do you do, sir," Casey said.

"*Physical* education, eh?" said Mr. Evans.

Naismith nodded and explained how word had already reached Springfield that Casey possessed the finest natural swing in all the world, more classic even than anything you could see in The League or The Association. "When the season is over," Naismith said, "if we were to send you a rail ticket, would you come out to Springfield someday and demonstrate your swing for the students?"

"Jeez, I don't know," Casey said, taken aback. "I haven't obtained a situation for the off-season yet, but the past two winters I traveled with the circus."

"Oh, I see," Naismith said, clearly disappointed.

Casey glanced over at Flossie out of the corner of his eye. " 'Course, I'm thinkin' now maybe I won't be leaving Mudville this fall," he said, and Flossie's heart bobbled a little at that piece of news.

"Well now," Naismith went on. "I think you'd be interested in what we do at the Training School. Besides baseball in the spring, we have gymnastics, swimming and football in the fall."

"What game do you play in the winter?" Casey asked.

"Nothing satisfactory yet, I'm afraid," Naismith replied. "But we're working on it."

Mr. Evans stepped up. "You know, Timothy, you're a bright lad and good at sport. Maybe you ought to think about *attending* that school over in Springfield after the season."

Casey gulped. "But that's a *college,* Mr. Evans, sir."

"There's no law says a ballist can't go to college, is there, Mr. Naismith?" And then he whirled on Flossie. "And you wouldn't mind being married to a college man, would you, Flossie?"

Casey's jaw dropped. Flossie shrieked, "Faith and begorra, sir," and dashed away. Mrs. Evans fumbled with the lemonade pitcher, trying to divert Naismith from these household goings-on. As for Casey, embarrassed though he was, still he had to laugh, and Mr. Evans threw an arm about him, more as if he were a son instead of some roisterous ballplayer. "A real nice piece of dry goods," Mr. Evans said, winking at Casey, as they watched Flossie's trim ship sail away. "A very nice piece of calico."

◆

Not only that, but a couple weeks later, just before Decoration Day, when Chester Drinkwater came by the big house on Elm Street with the mansard roof, Mr. Evans brought Casey right into the parlor with him. Equals all. It was even more ironic, too, because while Flossie was serving them tea, Flossie was exactly what Drinkwater had come to talk about. "Mr. Evans," he said, "would it be possible for Miss Cleary to come away with Mr. Casey and myself—and my spinster sister Maud, who will chaperone—and go down to visit Nantasket Beach on Thursday?"

No baseball clubs played seven days a week in those times. Even the National League couldn't schedule Sundays, which was maddening, because, of course, Sunday was the one day most cranks were off. The normal workday was ten and a half hours, Monday through Saturday, a sixty-three-hour week. There was the odd town here and there that didn't have Blue Laws, and such places automatically became prime franchise sites for minor-league clubs. But even then, many vigilant Americans—particularly the members of the American Sabbath Union, the Sunday League of America (which counted Mrs. Evans on its roster) and the Lord's Day Alliance—worked day in and day out (Sundays excepted, of course) to make sure that citizens took their one day off without enjoying saloons, baseball or trolley rides.

This particular week in the schedule, the last one in May, was an especially bountiful one for grumpy old Cyrus Weatherly because of the memorial holiday. He exploited Decoration Day fully, too, playing a doubleheader—separate admissions, of course, morning and afternoon, before and after the town parade. But after that the Mudville nine was off the next two days, till Saturday, so Casey had the opportunity to get to the beach.

"I've just taken a keen liking to this young man," Drinkwater said, patting Casey on the knee. "And the way baseball is taking hold nowadays, people have a notion to listen to the likes of Casey. There may be a lot of cranks out there who'd love to deal with a ballist like Timothy if he were a salesman for me in the off-season."

"Good business," said Mr. Evans.

"It'd sure be better than trying to lift that fat lady two, three times a day," Casey allowed.

Mr. Evans curled his mustache, thinking. "Well, as long as Flossie's chaperoned—"

"Oh yes indeed; as I said, my spinster sister Maud will—"

"—and as long as she can make up the time she misses, working her off-afternoons, I can't see why Flossie can't go with you and Casey and your spinster sister Maud to Nantasket."

"Oh, thank you, sir," Casey whooped, and he bolted into the kitchen to tell Flossie the good news, planting a big kiss on her right in front of Ida, the cook.

Mr. Evans turned back to his visitor. "You know, Mr. Drinkwater, I just can't tell you what a difference Casey has made to this little town of ours. Why, he's not only changed the whole spirit of Mudville, but he's got people going over to that old East Side again. Down at First F and M, we haven't had any interest in any property out there in years, but people go out to the Grounds, see Casey wallop one, and . . . all of a sudden I've got mortgage applications piling up on my desk for property out there. It's simply amazing what a baseball team can do for a town. Something new in our society. Quite extraordinary. Had you ever thought about that?"

"No, I never had," Chester Drinkwater said, lying through his teeth.

5

ONE FINE
DECORATION DAY

◆

Casey's Decoration Day performance was as superb as any hitter could have in any era: eight for eleven, two homers, ten RBIs. The Lynns had to go to their change pitcher in both games, but to no avail. And what crowds! SRO! Everybody waving American flags—all thirty-eight stars! Even some of the local swells snuck over from the horse show, and the children were hanging from the trees. For the afternoon game, the marching bands from the Decoration Day parade reassembled at the Grounds, so grumpy old Cyrus Weatherly let them sit behind a rope inside the center-field fence—for a dime a head—and they serenaded the crowd all afternoon, adding even more of a holiday air.

Mudville had never seen such crowds, and here it was still only May. Word about Mighty Casey had even reached to Boston, and since the Beaneaters were on a western swing, in Indianapolis, a few cranks even took the train out from the city. From Springfield, Jim Naismith came again, bringing a colleague, a tiny little fellow teacher named Amos Alonzo Stagg. Ernest Thayer, Harvard '85, a frustrated poet, who was resigned to working in the family wool business, traveled to Mudville from Worcester.

Flossie snuck away from the Evans house late in the day, and managed to get inside the Grounds for the last couple of innings. She had found a good view by the time Casey came to the bat for the last time on the day. It was the eighth inning. Hughie Barrows was on second and Johnny Flynn on first, and Casey took two strikes and then knocked them both in with a ground-rule double that rolled into a French horn in straightaway center field. The Grounds went berserk. The score didn't mean anything now. In fact, baseball didn't matter. It was mostly just a case of pride. The people of Mudville not only had a hero, but they were touched by him, even made heroic by him. If the Baron de Coubertin had been there that day, he might have right then scratched that idea he was working on about the modern Olympics. The athletes weren't really going to have all that much to do with it anymore. It went beyond them, out of their control. More and more, the spirit was going to be in the stands, with the cranks, in the city, with the people who read about the games in the papers or in Richard Fox's magazine. The spirit in the game wasn't ever again going to mean nearly so much as the spirit surrounding it.

But who could begin to sense that in 1888? Certainly, all Flossie could see was this glorious, innocent face on second base: Casey, standing there in his high-top spikes, his cap off, waving to the throng, beaming. Virtually all the ballists wore mustaches, and many of them bushy sideburns to boot. But Casey was apart, a beardless Alexander the Great midst all the older, hirsute generals. His face was as clean as it was bright, his eyes as clear blue as the best aggies that Mudville's marble-shooting kids favored, his hair the color of a base path, his uniform happily dirty—not poverty dirty or grubby dirty, but boyishly dirty, good dirty. God, but Casey was clean. The tears poured down Flossie's cheeks. She was so in love, and maybe even better, she knew that Casey loved her too.

In the stands back of third base, Ernest Thayer turned to a friend. "You know that song about King Kelly?" he asked.

"Sure: 'Slide, Kelly, Slide.' 'Slide, Kelly, slide. Slide, Kelly, on your belly. Slide, Kelly, slide.' "

"Hey, good. And there's the barroom rhyme for The Great John L.," Thayer said, and he cleared out his throat and recited, perfectly, from memory:

> "His colors are the Stars and Stripes.
> He also wears the green.
> And he's the greatest slugger that
> The ring has ever seen.

No fighter in the world can beat
Our true American.
The champion of all champions,
John L. Sullivan."

"Ace memory, Ernest."

"Yeah, well this fellow deserves even more. He deserves an epic poem. I think I'll come back out here Saturday."

"Are you kidding? Harvard plays Princeton Saturday."

Thayer shrugged. He would rather return to Mudville. On second base, Casey put his cap back on, and when he did, it was as if he caught a sunbeam in it, and the rays wreathed his head in amber. Then he hitched up his pants and took a long lead off second.

6

A STARTLING
CHANGE OF
CHAPERONES

Drinkwater escorted Flossie and Casey out of the Cyclorama. Her mind was still swimming at that marvel of this age, the grandest thing she had seen on either side of the Atlantic. And now Drinkwater took her by her elbow and helped her into his rig, a magnificent surrey drawn by two great matching chestnuts. Why, Cinderella herself hadn't gone to the ball in anything finer.

Flossie waited then for Drinkwater to climb in, but, instead, to her surprise, he closed the door on Casey and herself. "Now, Rooney'll get you safely to my boat at Hingham Bay, don't you worry," he said.

Flossie shot a quick look at Casey. What sort of strumpet did he think she was, going off to Nantasket Beach alone with a man? Mercifully, though, Flossie could read just as much confusion on Casey's face. "But, Mr. Drinkwater, Mr. Evans wouldn't let Flossie go unless you accompanied us," Casey sputtered.

"And your spinster sister Maud, as my chaperone!" Flossie cried out.

"Now, now, dear," Drinkwater said, raising his hand and fluttering it to signal them to calm down. "We've had just a bit of a change. Maud has a touch of the vapors, it seems, and so I've pressed my spinster niece Phoebe into service as the chaperone. Phoebe won't be free until somewhat later in the day, so I certainly didn't want you to miss the opportunity to partake of bathing on the beach. I've hired another rig, and Phoebe and I will join you in Nantasket in time for dinner."

"Ah, sir, but—" Flossie began, absolutely delighted to have Casey all to herself, but mortified to think that she might possibly reveal that attitude.

"Don't you worry, Miss Cleary. Rooney here is the very soul of propriety," said Drinkwater, and put his bowler on and tapped it, indicating that this conversation was concluded. "Double back by The Common before you head south," Drinkwater called up to Rooney. "I want all of Boston to see such pulchritude adorning my rig." And for good

Drinkwater and Phoebe
"chaperoned" Casey and Flossie
at the beach—but whose eyes
were on whom?

War—and that didn't even begin to take into account the trolley suburbs. Not so long ago, a city was realistically defined by how far a person could walk, from home to work and back again, to the market and the church and the whiskey hole, but now there were two hundred and thirty-one miles of trolley lines in and around Boston, transporting eighty-five million passengers a year; all manner of human souls: Chinamen with pigtails, Jews with funny beards, Poles and Gypsies, Negroes shining black as coal, sailors and fishermen, stinking of cod, ragpickers, beggars and urchins, and (some) terribly wicked women. Almost three quarters of the city was immigrant or first generation. Why, since '85 Boston had even had an Irish mayor, so now the Micks could comfortably look down on the Dagos up in the North End, just as the hoity-toity Back Bay Yankees had always sneered at them. Last one off the boat is a . . . What else could hold this disjointed, eccentric mass together but churches, saloons and baseball?

Rooney reined in the surrey by The Common to let a trolley flash by, the passengers hanging on, hanging out the sides, jaunty in the warm air. Tomorrow would be June, summer seemed early this year, and Casey and his beautiful lady were going to the beach, no less! Rooney took them this way and that. Oh, the theaters! The Howard! The Bijou! Ullie Akerstrom herself was starring in *Annette, the Dancing Girl,* and, even more impressive, at The Boston Museum, the fabled Richard Mansfield was in a tour de force: matinees of *Prince Karl,* evenings playing the title roles of *Dr. Jekyll and Mr. Hyde*. And the shops: magnificent suits and gowns, hats—

measure, he winked, as Rooney clucked at the pair of chestnuts and pulled away.

Flossie turned to Casey. "Are you truly sure about Mr. Drinkwater's scruples, Timothy?"

Casey snapped his arms folded across his chest. "Why the deuce must you be such a crosspatch about Mr. Drinkwater?"

"Oh, I don't know. I—I—I just worry about him."

"Please don't," Casey said, turning to her and looking directly into her eyes. "Please. Trust me." And Flossie nodded she would, not necessarily because she did, but because something much more important suddenly occurred to her. It was this: when she had slid over to let Chester Drinkwater in the rig, he didn't get in, only she had never slid back (in all the confusion), so here she was now, brazenly riding along in downtown Boston, as big as life, her body *touching a member of the opposite gender*. Even worse—even better—her body touching Timothy F. X. Casey.

But then, after due consideration, Flossie decided she would remain brazen, and stayed right where she was.

Besides: what a ride! Flossie had been in the big city before, even lived there briefly when she first arrived from Ireland, but this was different, riding along in this magnificent rig, behind these two great chestnuts, Casey beside her, the world at their feet, the two of them looking down on the eclectic humanity scrambling all about them.

Boston had exploded into a city of four hundred thousand people, easily double what it had been at the time of the Civil *chapeaux!*—and the most glorious shawls in the Jordan Marsh window, on sale for $2.25. Hang the outrageous price—how Flossie wanted one. But there was no time and so much to see. Rooney headed south, toward Dorchester.

"Perhaps I shall make you a sweater for your birthday," Flossie said.

"A what now do you say? Sweat-tore?"

"A sweater. It's a new garment for gentlemen, and I should love to see you in one," Flossie cooed, and it was all she could do to restrain herself from snuggling up closer.

Just then, though, she spied a billiard parlor across the way, and it made her flush. Even a nice girl like Flossie knew that a billiard parlor on the ground floor meant a bordello above. Luckily, Casey didn't see it. He was glancing the other way, at the large apothecary on the corner.

In an up-to-date place like Boston, druggists were everywhere, curing most all the sundry ails of mankind. Signs proclaimed nostrums to correct: Obesity! (Stout People Need Not Despair Any Longer!) Unfortunate Posture! Opium Addiction! The Ill Effects of Youthful Errors! Diminished Vigor! Summer Debilities! Lost Manhood! Early Decay! And there was something for everyone: Dr. Carter's Little Female Pills! Lydia Pinkham's Famous Vegetable Compound for Women! Unrivalled Eureka Pills for Weak Men!

Flossie shook her head. Why, the way things were going, what in the world would doctors do with themselves in the twentieth century?

And there, over there, over that way, Flossie saw a tramp wearing a sandwich board that exalted Turkish Hair Tonic.

So, playfully, she tugged at Casey's locks. Oops, she shouldn't have done that, because on the other side of the board the product advertised was Prof. F. C. Foster's Bust Developer—Five Inches Guaranteed! And so Casey paid her back by pointing wickedly at Flossie's chest, making her blush to beat the band.

But there were so many more sights rolling by. And if there was one thing promised more than wonder cures, it was peeks into the future. Clairvoyants were, it seemed, on every block. Minnie Day! Card Reading a Specialty! Arabella Page and Her Clairvoyant Massage Treatment! Eureka Modern Palmism! Madame Iris: Electric Treatments to See the Future! Samantha Dolan and Her Amazing Magnetic Methods! Flossie was suitably impressed by all these seers, but, she thought, could the future possibly ever be any more exciting than this glorious day today, Thursday, May the 31st, eighteen hundred and eighty-eight? How could it ever be any better? Ever?

And thinking just that, Flossie made the mistake of turning to Casey and looking at him, and because Casey could tell the present, he felt her stare and sensed her joy, and he turned to her.

How soft Flossie looked to him. How adorable. Casey even had to swallow a little. How smooth was her face—and in a world where so many people had the pox marks, Flossie's own countenance seemed all the more polished, even lapidary, the rosy cheeks blushing, the green eyes enraptured, the tendrils of hair falling gently across her forehead. Flossie knew Casey was going to embrace her then, kiss her right there in the surrey, in the sunlight, and she also knew she wasn't going to stop him, and, yes indeed, when Casey didn't disappoint, when he took her in his arms and pressed his lips against hers, Flossie fell onto him and kissed him back with every bit as much fervor.

It absolutely astonished Casey, and so it was he, finally, who pulled back, wide-eyed. "You're as beautiful as Frances Folsom herself," he gasped at last—the ultimate compliment.

Flossie's mother had told her about boys like this. "Am I now?"

"Oh yes, only I'm sure she doesn't kiss the President nearly so well," and he smirked, making Flossie duck her head in proud embarrassment.

When she looked up, she knew Casey was going to kiss her again, and so, to stop this utter madness, she put a finger to his lips. "No, no more, Timothy. We're not betrothed."

"Oh, and would you want to be betrothed to a ballist?" Flossie did exactly the right thing. She ducked her head and didn't say a word, so Casey had to go on. "I mean, I don't even know where I'll be next summer. Not in Mudville, for sure. I hope someplace in The League or The Association, but it could be another minor club . . . somewhere."

"Oh, and is that so important now? It wasn't so long ago that I was in another country, and then I came on the boat to America and there I was all by meself in Boston."

"What did you do?"

"Took on as a seamstress, I did. Eleven hours for two and a half, all hunched over"—Flossie pantomimed sewing—

"and I saw some of the older lasses already wearing blue glasses, their eyes deteriorating from the work, and I said to meself, Florence, this is no better than bein' in Ireland, back in Cork with no work a'tall, so when a girl friend told me about maybe being a maid, I examined that situation."

"And that's how you came to Mudville?"

"Aye. And where was that to me? So I'm not beyond taking up and leaving again, either." And Casey did exactly the right thing. He ducked his head and didn't say a word, so Flossie had to go on. "I mean, of course, were there good reason, of course. Now understand, Mudville is a lovely place and Mr. and Mrs. Evans are—"

Casey was kind enough to save her any more babbling embarrassment. He suddenly raised up, then leaned forward and poked the driver. "Rooney, stop—over there," he called, and he pointed across the street to a sign: "PRINCESS CLARA, CLAIRVOYANT EXTRAORDINAIRE . . . The Future Revealed with the New Amazing Electric Belt!"

Rooney steered over. Flossie shook her head. "Timothy F. X. Casey, not on your life. I shan't do it!"

Casey shrugged. "Then I shall," he said, and climbed out of his side of the surrey. Flossie pouted a bit more, but then she came after him, and, together, they entered Princess Clara's mysterious chambers. It was a small room, and, really, hardly different from any Victorian parlor—dark, clingy, full of bric-a-brac, dripping with fringe. Princess Clara fit in neatly with these surroundings, with clothes that more or less matched the furnishings. She clasped her bejeweled hands and cooed at her customers.

"Ahh, my dearie," she said to Flossie, "come to have your fortune told, have you?"

"No, not the lady," Casey said. "Me."

"Ah, so much the better, I should peer into the mind of such a fair young man." And she winked at Flossie and steered Casey over to the other side of the room, where she pushed him down onto the divan. Then she brought out a leather belt that was attached to a wire. "The amazing electric belt that reveals the future," Princess Clara said by way of explanation.

"You can't see the future without it?" Flossie asked.

"Oh no, dearie. A person must be born with the art of clairvoyance. The amazing electric belt only helps me see ahead more clearly. Some days, when the electricity is cleanest, I can see well into the twentieth century." Flossie gasped. "Once, last February, I saw all the way to 1911."

Princess Clara put the belt about Casey and plugged it in. *Voilà!* One little light went on. Casey and Flossie both gasped. For people only just now getting used to electricity, this was positively incredible. Then Princess Clara ran another wire to some sort of gaudy tiara that she placed on her own head, sat down next to Casey and took his hands.

"This isn't . . . dangerous, is it?" he inquired.

"Only if I see dangerous things ahead for you. But wait, wait . . ." Princess Clara closed her eyes. "Now I see only happiness for you. Pleasure, fun, relaxation, water . . . lots of water—"

"Yes, yes, we're going bathing at Nantasket Beach," Flossie blurted out.

"Ah, as I said." Princess Clara sighed, leaning back for the moment, resting from her arduous psychic labors. Considering that they were already in Quincy, on the shore road, the princess was not exactly going out on a limb, but Casey shook his head in admiring awe no less than Flossie, and they exchanged the fondest of looks. Quickly, then, Princess Clara put her hand to her temple. "And love!" she called out, trilling. "Love is in the air, all about you, sir. It's even making the electricity jiggle." Flossie blushed, and Casey swelled up, proud that his emotions could actually get the best of electricity itself.

"What about my future at work?" Casey asked.

Uh oh. Her clairvoyant highness was struggling here. This fellow looked like just another laborer, a powerful Mick, and this was surely just some mouse of an Irish maid that he was with, but his hands weren't callused the way they should be, and although he was clearly right-handed, it was the left one that was rough. And besides, he had such bearing, this chap. "It's blurry, blurry," Princess Clara said, covering her eyes, readjusting her tiara.

"Mr. Casey is a great ballist, you know," Flossie said.

Princess Clara opened her eyes and turned to Flossie. "Please, dearie, I cannot see into the future if you interrupt me," she said sharply, and Flossie mumbled an apology. Then Princess Clara went back to concentrating. "Now, now, I see something. It's green, and it's a great place, and I see many, many people."

"Incredible," Casey said. "That would be the Grounds, on Saturday."

"Yes, it is." She pressed her temple again, and this time her eyes flew open wide, and she turned to Casey, and with much more authority in her voice, she spoke up: "I can see so clearly now. So clearly. You are the hero. You—"

"How many hits do I get? Do I get a homer?"

"A homer?" Her royal psychic obviously didn't know baseball from botany, which, in a way, made her efforts now to see the future all the more impressive. "I don't know the term. . . . I just see everyone cheering and your team wins and you are the hero."

"I must hit a home run," Casey said, leaning back.

"Sorry, I really don't know," Princess Clara said. "But I do know that'll be twenty-five cents."

Casey dug into his pocket. "Wait," Flossie said. "I just have one more question about Mr. Casey's future."

"All right, dearie, for another half-a-dime."

"Just tell me what's going to happen in his dealings with Mr. Chester Drinkwater."

"Well now, let me see," Princess Clara said, fixing her tiara again, but before the electricity had a chance to flow from the future into the amazing electric belt, Casey had ripped it off, slapped down a quarter and started for the door. "Damnit to hell, Florence Cleary, I told you to stop asking those questions," he snapped, and then he stomped off to the surrey. He was so peeved at Flossie, he sulked intermittedly for the rest of the trip, or, anyway, until they put on their bathing costumes at Nantasket Beach and Casey actually got to see the flesh of Flossie's incredibly erotic ankles.

A RANCOROUS TELEPHONE CALL

Richard Fox alighted at Boston's new Park Square Terminal that afternoon. What a ride it had been: highballing almost all the way, mile-a-minute, throttle out, a sumptuous meal, exquisite comfort and service. The porter had even pressed Fox's new thirty-dollar whiskey-shade suit and supplied him with another boutonniere, so he was fresh as a daisy when he arrived in Beantown. How many times had Fox advised friends: Whatever you do, whatever the market does, don't sell your railroad stock.

At the Parker House his suite was ready (of course), but telephones had not yet been installed in guest rooms, and so, while a bellboy took his bag up, Fox went over to the telephone traffic operator and asked her to ring him up a local number.

The hello girl called 247, which was the number of the Third Base Saloon at 940 Columbus Avenue. Fox picked up the receiver, and after a moment a man's voice came on. "Hello" was what it said. Since people were new to phones then, they didn't answer by saying who they were. They didn't say "Third Base Saloon." They still just said "Hello," as people had been greeting others down through all previous human history.

"I'd like to talk to Mr. McGreevey, please," Fox said.

"Yeah, this is McGreevey. This is Nuf Ced. And who might you be?"

"This is Richard Fox . . . of *The Police Gazette*."

There was a pause on the other end, and then the man clearly let fly into a spittoon. *'Pit-too.* "I don't know if I wanna talk to ya."

"Is Sullivan there?"

"Maybe he is. Maybe he isn't."

"Look, Nuf Ced, I'm trying to make a lot of money for Sullivan. Tell 'im I came to Boston, and—"

'Pit-too. "Johnny ain't in Boston."

"So, when's he get back?"

"Maybe tomorrow." *'Pit-too.* "Maybe not."

"Okay, you just tell The Big Fellow that I'll be at your place tomorrow night."

"Aye, I'll tell 'im." *'Pit-too.* "But I ain't sayin' Johnny'll like it any, Fox. 'Nough said?" said Nuf Ced.

THE GRAND SHOW
AT NANTASKET

The reason The Great John L. wasn't in Boston that Thursday was because it was he who was the feature attraction of the Nantasket Beach show that evening. Why should he defend his title against Jake Kilrain when he could make a king's ransom walking through exhibitions?

For the show, Chester Drinkwater had obtained the choicest seats for Flossie and Casey and for himself and his spinster niece Phoebe, who was, of course, substituting as chaperone for his spinster sister Maud. Truth to tell, though, Phoebe didn't look much like a chaperone. In fact, the first thing that passed through Flossie's mind when she met Phoebe at dinner was: "She certainly doesn't look like a chaperone."

The first thing that passed through Casey's mind on this same occasion was: "She certainly doesn't look like a spinster."

Phoebe was perhaps a few years older than Flossie, but the dappled aura of sophistication hung on her no less than the men did. Many of those in the dining room even seemed to know Drinkwater's niece as well as they knew Drinkwater himself. And he was a very well known man. Guests kept coming over to the table. "Chester, what a swell trolley deal in West Roxbury." And: "The situation for electric streetcars in Pawtucket appears ideal right now, Mr. D." And: "If we were to run a new line in the north of Natick, I think we could put an amusement park out there." And so on and so forth.

Flossie kept her eyes on Drinkwater, if not, perhaps, quite as much as Phoebe kept her hands on Casey. Worse than that, how raggedy Flossie felt beside Phoebe! Here Flossie was decked out in her very best Sunday gingham, and it looked absolutely tawdry compared to Phoebe's magnificent brown foulard gown, with white polka dots, and a bonnet and parasol to match. No wonder the men stared at Phoebe so. No wonder Casey did. Phoebe didn't look at all like a chaperone. Flossie was relieved when dinner was finished, and they could finally get out of the glare of the dining room and get over to the pavilion, under the soft colored lanterns, to see the show.

And what a performance it was! As much as Flossie had

Saloon-keeper McGreevey,
better known as Nuf Ced, standing
before the Third Base Saloon

believed that nothing on God's green earth could ever possibly compare to the Gettysburg Cyclorama, Nantasket offered a plethora of first-class entertainment the likes of which could certainly not exist anywhere else in the world. Here was the bill:

First, Gardini and Hamlet, black-face singers. Then, the solemn dramatic recitations of Amos P. Lawrence, followed by John Mahoney, who did a "laughable trapeze," adroitly mixing humor with danger. Jessie Allyne came next, a brief novelty act. She let her magnificent hair down and down . . . and down, until the golden tresses lay in great coiled rings at her feet. "I seen something like that in a sideshow once," Casey said, "but the lady in question wasn't nearly so grand." This was followed by The Authentic Monkey Orchestra, and then Fairfax and Siegfried, human statues extraordinaire. "You can't see them move a muscle," Flossie said. "They don't even blink," Casey added. The finale of this portion of the show was the ever popular Willie Arnold, "New England's favorite jig dancer"—and anybody could see why.

Then it was time for the fisticuffs. But first, before John L. came on, Patsey Kerrigan and George LaBlanche fought under the old ring rules, which the announcer explained meant "anything but biting." It was well known that Sullivan himself would have none of that anymore. It was odd about him. As utterly crude as he was, almost barbaric in his habits, he preferred gloves and the new, more refined Marquess of Queensberry rules, with scoring by rounds of "scientific points." Sullivan fought all his exhibitions that way and didn't want to go bare-knuckle again, even if that was still the vogue and very much what the hard-core *Police Gazette* readers cottoned to. For that matter, even the fashionable Nantasket crowd showed a certain primeval fascination as Kerrigan and LaBlanche clawed one another.

Drinkwater leaned across Phoebe to Casey. "Look about," he said. "Look at your Miss Cleary and my, uh, niece here—look all around and you'll espy that much of the applause here comes from the dainty gloved hands." Casey nodded. "You see, Timothy, if the fairer sex can favor a raw free-for-all as we've just seen, think how many of the lovelies would be attracted to a fine, clean sporting event like baseball"—and he lifted a finger—"particularly if it were played in a better part of town."

Casey started to approve this wisdom, but he was stopped cold, for at that moment, The Great John L. entered the stage, a huge emerald-green robe slung loosely over his shoulders, the championship belt about his waist. Casey was absolutely aghast. The Boston Strong Boy was, in fact, The Boston Fat Boy. "He's fat," Flossie said, with shock.

"Disgustingly fat," said Phoebe, with disgust.

The fat rolled over John L., tumbling over the belt so that many of the 397 diamonds were obscured by his avoirdupois. The heavyweight champion of the world, twenty-nine years old, looked closer to thirty-nine, packing two hundred and fifty flabby pounds on his five-foot-ten-and-a-half-inch frame. He was grotesque. Even the toadies around him couldn't avoid the obvious and had started referring to him, delicately, as The Big Fellow.

Sullivan's attendant, a spidery little sort named Smiler

Pippen, laced on the champ's gloves, and that minimum of motion was enough to jiggle Sullivan's jowls and belly. John L. liked having Smiler around, because his training regimen pleased the champ. Smiler demanded that Sullivan deny himself liquor and cigars for whole hours at a time, that he partake of leisurely strolls, and that, upon his return, he receive a rubdown and a large dosage of Smiler's own physic, so called, which was made up of zinnia, salts and licorice. With a general aversion to all forms of labor, Sullivan swore by this routine.

Now he sauntered out to face off with one Francis Sheehan, and Casey, to his surprise, discovered that Sullivan could be remarkably nimble when he had to . . . for four or five seconds. But he was much too much the walrus to maintain any pace, and although his blows obviously devastated poor Sheehan every time they landed, Sullivan rarely had the energy or position to toss one. Hardly was it a scintillating climax to *le programme,* and when the "referee" lifted John L's hand in victory, the applause was but modest, and Drinkwater and his guests departed a bit disappointed.

Casey had hoped for a stroll down the boardwalk, perhaps even a little trip along the beach, he and Flossie dipping their toes in the surf, but she was exhausted from the long day, and he had to settle for a chaste peck on her cheek. Phoebe stepped forward then, conscientiously assumed her chaperone's mantle and ushered Flossie off to her room.

As Casey watched the ladies depart, Drinkwater came up and clapped him on the shoulder. "What dya say, a little nose paint?" he asked, beckoning to the gentlemen's bar.

That sounded good to Casey, and they took a table, and brandies and cigars. Drinkwater let the smoke curl over his mustache. "Well, Timothy, my boy," he said, "have you decided to accept my little proposition?"

If only Flossie could have been a fly on the wall! She was absolutely right in suspecting some monkey business between her Casey and Chester Drinkwater.

"I think so," Casey began uneasily. "But I'm not—"

"I understand. You're a prudent young man," Drinkwater said, toasting him. "So, we'll run over it again." He drummed his fingers together. "Now, you tell me you make—"

"Eight hundred dollars—"

"—playing for Mudville." And, with that, Drinkwater took out his billfold and laid down eight one-hundred-dollar bills. Casey blinked. "And, if you stay, you'll be reserved. You understand that? They'll own you. Reserve is just a pretty word for own. Bad enough the sonsuvbitches who own baseball teams put that provision in for the major club players, but now it's going in the minors, too. What is this? Slavery? This is 1888, Timothy. We fought a war over this twenty-five years ago."

"Yes sir." The nerve of grumpy old Cyrus Weatherly and those other owners!

"Now, *I'm* prepared to pay you three thousand dollars"— and to spell things out, Drinkwater laid down two more centuries and two thousand-dollar bills. Casey gasped. "That's just mad money. Nothing to it. Just leave Mudville, clear out, take the summer off. Next summer, you'll be as free as a bird, and then, Timothy, my boy, I'll help you sign with anyone."

"The Beaneaters."

"No, I'd advise against that. King Kelly'd be so jealous of you, you'd regret it. His Highness always needs to be the big toad in the puddle. So think long about that. But how about New York . . . or Detroit, Washington—or Pittsburgh? Oh yeah, wouldn't that Billy Sunday love to have you batting behind him in the lineup instead of those lulus and cakes they've got there now!"

Casey's eyes twinkled, but Drinkwater wasn't through. "And finally," he said, "just to seal the bargain, an extra five hundred dollars," and he laid out a five-hundred-dollar bill. "And I'll throw in a beautiful new gown for that young lady of yours, too. I could see her eyeing Phoebe's. You get this right now"—and he slid the bill closer to Casey—"and the rest after five more games."

"And all I have to do is make outs."

"That's right. I don't want you making another hit. I don't want you just disappearing now. That'd be too curious. But you haven't struck out all year, and if all of a sudden the Mighty Casey starts fanning, it'll really break some hearts. Then you take the three thousand dollars and drop out of sight—only when you materialize next year, you'll be with some major club."

Casey's hand itched to reach out and take the $500, but, at the last, he grabbed the brandy glass instead. Casey was no dummy. "Mr. Drinkwater, I'm no dummy," he said by way of explanation. "There must be a reason you'd pay me all this money not to do *anything*."

"Of course there is, my boy. But there's a new expression

going round. Maybe you've heard it: What you don't know won't hurt you." Casey nodded. "But you have my word as a sporting man that it's not illegal. Nothing against the law. So, what dya say?" And Drinkwater raised his brandy glass.

Casey paused and looked long at the glass. "I say, lemme sleep on it."

"Very wise of you, my boy," Drinkwater said, chuckling. "Very wise. Yes indeed, you get up to your room and you sleep on it tonight. Heh, heh."

9

A CONSIDERABLE SURPRISE

Casey entered his room. Right away, Phoebe came toward him from out of the shadows, letting her long sable hair tumble down to the brown foulard dress with the white polka dots. Only that was when Casey realized that she didn't have the brown foulard dress with the white polka dots on anymore. "I thought you'd never come up, Timothy," Phoebe sighed, moving close and putting her hot lips on his.

Then she seduced him.

When Phoebe dressed, she pulled a five-hundred-dollar bill out of her purse and left it on the bedside table. "So, we're in business with my, uh, Uncle Chester," she said. And Casey smiled and nodded. Phoebe blew him a kiss, and then closed the door softly behind her.

Casey watched her go. He felt rotten, dirty and deceitful, and wondered how soon before he could see her again.

10

FLOSSIE PUTS HER FOOT DOWN

L ate the next afternoon, Friday, back in Boston, Casey and Flossie strolled along the broad esplanade by the Charles River. They'd come up from Nantasket with Phoebe and Drinkwater and were going to spend the night at the Parker House and enjoy a gay evening on the town before heading out to Mudville the next morning and the big game against Lynn. It was a glorious day, the grass emerald, the sculls and sails upon the water, the swells from the Back Bay in all their finest finery promenading

. . . but Casey knew that none of those ladies, no one in all of Boston, was so gorgeous that day as his Flossie.

Drinkwater had arranged for there to be a whole new fancy outfit waiting for her at the hotel: blue-and-white-striped silk, it was, wide cuffs and a deep collar of white linen, topped by a leghorn straw sailor with a blue band and a flowing white ribbon. Flossie's full bosom filled her dress like one of those sails on the Charles, going with the wind, her matching parasol a spinnaker behind. "You're the loveliest of all, Flossie," Casey said. "There's not a man on the esplanade who's not trying to catch your eye."

"Fiddle-faddle. No one would buck a gentleman so pleasing to the eye as *you*. Why, when I was at The Grounds on Decoration Day, I heard one man say you would soon be as good as King Kelly himself, and his lady friend said that was no mind to her, because you were already better-looking than His Highness." And Flossie flipped her parasol a little as she said that. She was learning quickly how much more effectively she could flirt when she was dressed more expensively. "But, ah, I must be watching you, I must."

"What?" said Casey, still ruminating about being better-looking than King Kelly. After all, His Royal Highness wasn't just regarded as the handsomest ballist, but as the handsomest man.

"I said: I must be watching you. I must," Flossie repeated, more emphatically, and she stopped her walk to punctuate the statement.

"Oh, and how's that?"

"That Phoebe woman. I truly do not believe that she's Mr.

Drinkwater's niece, but I most certainly do believe she'd like nothing better than to seduce you, Timothy Casey."

Casey threw his hands to his head and rolled his eyes. "Flossie, that is the most ridiculous thing I've ever heard," he said, and he shook his head for effect and stared out at the river. *Whew,* he thought, *I nipped that in the bud.*

Ohhh, no, thought Flossie, *she's seduced him already.*

So she turned to face him squarely. "You made your deal with Mr. Chester Drinkwater, didn't you now?"

"Sure enough," Casey said, beaming, pulling out the five-hundred-dollar bill and brandishing it, then telling her all the benign details of the arrangement. But Flossie turned away when he told her he was going to leave the Mudville nine after a few games of batting poorly, and she wouldn't even look back at him, although he came up behind her and laid his hands on her waist and told her about how now he'd have enough money to marry her . . . "if only you'd have me."

Flossie bit her lip. How long she had waited to hear those words. But she would not turn around. "I love you, Timothy. I surely do. But I can't be marryin' you if you're involved in—"

Casey took his hands off her waist and ran around Flossie to look her in the eye. "But, Flossie, Flossie darling, there's nothing illegal. I promise you that. Be practical. This is 1888 now. I told—"

"Well let me tell you," Flossie snapped, her green eyes searing. "Mudville loves you as I do, Mr. Casey. You have taken that ball team and changed the entire spirit of the town. Why, I've heard Mr. Evans tell others that you're bringin' the whole

East Side to life by yourself, you are. And can't you see what Mr. Drinkwater and that wicked lady who is not his niece want? They want to build a trolley line way out west of Mudville, practically to Devonbury, move everything out there. Can't you understand what he'll do to Mudville?"

Flossie stamped her parasol on the walk as if it were a shillelagh. "Timothy Casey, would you just be a dumb Mick? Can't you see? Why, I'll wager that Mr. Drinkwater's already bought up every piece of real estate out that way. It wouldn't surprise me if he's going to build an amusement park out there too, and even a . . . another baseball grounds. Can't you see that?"

"Listen, Flossie, I—"

"No. There is no listenin' for me. You breathed life into our little town, and now that man is stealin' you from us, he is. And that's worse than breakin' any law. Ah, that's breakin' the spirit."

"But, darling—" And Casey made the mistake of holding up the five-hundred-dollar bill, and when he did, Flossie slapped it away, and he had to scramble down the esplanade after it, chasing it in the wind, so that by the time he finally retrieved it and looked up, Flossie was already disappearing down the esplanade, her parasol furled, her pace determined, weaving in and out amongst the strollers.

11

OFF TO THE THIRD BASE SALOON

W hen Casey got back to the Parker House, there was a package waiting for him at the bell stand. He opened it up, and there, neatly laid out, was Flossie's gorgeous new dress. A note was pinned to it. "Dear Timothy [it read], I'm sorry, but I cannot accept this or accept what you are doing with yourself. Do not come calling on me again in any circumstance. Very truly yours, Florence M. Cleary."

Casey crumpled up the note in anger, hurled it away and rushed over to the desk. A well-dressed man in a whiskey-shade suit with a horseshoe pin on his cravat was standing there. He looked over Casey, looked back over to the dress laid out in the box. "Woman trouble?" he asked, but sympathetically, just-between-us-boys.

Still, Casey ignored him. "What room is Miss Phoebe Alexander in, please?" he inquired of the clerk at the desk.

"Seven-eighteen," said the clerk, and Casey grabbed a pen, splashed it into the inkwell, dashed off a note, and hollered for a bellboy.

"I'm sorry," said the man with the horseshoe pin, "I didn't mean to bother you, but you look like a boxer."

"A fighter? No, not me. I'm a ballist."

"Oh well, I'm sorry. It's just that you've got the build of a fighter, and I'm a fancy man myself." He put out his hand. "Richard Fox of *The Police Gazette*."

"No fooling," Casey said, licking the envelope. "Gee, I read *The Gazette* every month." He handed the bellboy the note and half-a-dime for a tip. "Seven-eighteen. And wait for the lady's reply." Then he stuck out his hand to Fox. "I'm Timothy Casey, rightfielder on the Mudville nine."

"Well, well," said Fox. "I've got a bit of business in a while, and it could only be a beautiful lady indeed to deserve such a gown, but if you're not joining her straightaway, perhaps you'd share some nose paint with me?"

"It is quite a beautiful lady," Casey said softly, but almost to himself. He looked at Fox. *The Police Gazette*. He looked over at the bellboy waiting for the elevator, and he saw Phoebe's hair cascading over her bare shoulders. He looked back at Fox. And now he saw eyes. Eyes flashed before his mind. But they were green. They were Flossie's eyes. He shook his head. He looked back to the bellboy. The door was opening. "Going up." He saw all of Flossie. The bellboy was getting on the elevator. Then he saw Flossie's love and his own shame—and in the split second it takes a horsehide to travel fifty feet to the bat, Casey dashed to the elevator and yanked the little bellboy out of its closing doors. "Keep the half-a-dime, but gimme the note back," he said, and then, smiling, he hustled over to Fox. "First round's on me," Casey said.

◆

Nobody had come up with the term "sports bar" in 1888, but had they, the Third Base Saloon, Michael T. McGreevey, Prop., would surely have been recognized as the first such institution. Athletic souvenirs—especially baseball gear, including a nearly idolatrous plaque of King Kelly by the front door—cluttered the place, barely leaving room for the cranks who jammed in, particularly after Beaneater games at the South End Grounds, just a skip away. "I call it Third Base 'cause it's the last place you go before you steal home," McGreevey would growl. " 'Nough said?"

He was stout and tiny, a terrier among men, with a handlebar mustache and a penchant for tending bar, going to games and swimming—something he did virtually every day of his life, so long as he could crack the ice. And, while he'd been baptized Michael Thomas, there wasn't a soul in all of Christendom who didn't call McGreevey Nuf Ced.

Fox explained this to Casey as they entered the Third

CASEY ON THE LOOSE

Base, trodding across the large mosaic on the floor, which spelled out "NUF CED." "He's here, Johnny," Nuf Ced roared from behind the bar.

"Who's here?" the great booming voice of John L. Sullivan answered from somewhere in the back. "Anybody important?"

"Aww, no. Just Richard Fox of *The Police Gazette,* the chucklehead who gave a championship belt to Jake Kilrain." *'Pit-too.*

Fox smiled facetiously, tipping his hat to Nuf Ced, and then he waved gaily toward wherever Sullivan might be. Then Fox and Casey took a table and ordered two bumpers of beer, and Fox explained that they would just have to cool their heels until it was Sullivan's pleasure to deign and see them. "So you've never thought about being a pugilist yourself," Fox said to Casey when the beers came.

"Not on your life; I can't abide fighting. That's not to say I haven't gotten my licks in, though. I hate to tell you this, but even in the national game some of the boys don't act like Americans. We only have the one umpire, you know, so some players'll grab you, step on your toe, slide right into your whiskers—and you have to paste 'em back. But it isn't to my liking."

"I'd hate to live in this republic if boys didn't put their dukes up," Fox said. "Puny dyspeptics with colossal heads never preserved a nation."

"Maybe not," Casey said, "but the ones who pick fights are the wrong ones to lead. You know, I've never seen a tough who wasn't a coward or a coward who wasn't a tough."

King Kelly
*wasn't just regarded as
the handsomest ballist, but the
handsomest man*

Barely as Casey got the last word in, there was a resounding thud, and his eyes shot up to see Sullivan standing there—having just slammed down a tankard of ale to introduce himself. The Big Fellow was accompanied by Smiler Pippen on the one side and his chippy of the evening, Rosie, on the other.

Fox nodded, barely, a greeting. Casey didn't. He only intently brushed the drops of beer that had splashed him off of his sleeve, and then blotted it with his handkerchief.

Only then did he look back up at Sullivan. And what he saw was something of a surprise. Casey had been in the very first row at Nantasket the night before, where the sight of the whole huge man had overwhelmed him. Now the certain parts came more into focus, and Casey was nearly fascinated at how white was John L.'s skin. It seemed almost alabaster, and against that paleness his black and smoldering eyes were set off even more. Sullivan picked his tankard back up off the table and slopped down a big swallow, and Casey was even more taken by his hands. They were peculiarly small— who ever would have thought it?—and, to boot, perfectly manicured, even pinkish. But Sullivan didn't offer a hand to shake. Instead, he just snarled: "All right, Fox, what is it you're wantin' now?"

Nuf Ced took his cue, spit, and came out from behind the bar. He headed over to the table, between the two men. Everybody else in the Third Base fell silent. Sullivan took out a big cigar, spit out the end and turned to Smiler for a light.

"I just want you to fight Kilrain for the championship, Johnny."

Sullivan blew some smoke. "Fight him for you, Fox? I ain't no henhouse to let a Fox into," he bellowed, and the whole Third Base roared at The Big Fellow's wit.

"Okay, fine, then don't let me be involved," Fox went on. "Just fight 'im. That's what all the fancy wants. . . . Or are you too fat now, Johnny? Too old?"

"Why you goddamn—" and Sullivan reached down to grab Fox, his hand going straight for the throat, right at the tie with the diamond horseshoe pin. He'd taken the bait. Fox had figured that Nuf Ced would jump right in to save him, and that's exactly what he did, but what Fox didn't figure was that even faster still, his new friend Casey would spring to his feet. Casey did. Not only that, before anyone knew what had happened, Casey had shoved John L. Sullivan. His ale went flying and his cigar fell from his chops, and he staggered back two or three steps before—with the help of Smiler and Rosie—he regained his balance. "Why you little—"

But Nuf Ced jumped into his path. " 'Nough said, Johnny," he shouted. And then, turning back to Fox, pointing a finger at him: " 'Nough said. There's no fightin' in my whiskey hole."

Sullivan nodded, but he stepped forward, brushing Nuf Ced aside so that he stood directly before Casey. "Fine, but who the hell are you, sonny?" And he glared at Casey.

Casey didn't back down. Not an inch. Indeed, he leaned forward a little and never took his eyes off John L. "My name is Timothy F. X. Casey," he said, "and I can beat any sonuvabitch in the house."

The entire Third Base Saloon fell into a hush. "Is he serious?" Sullivan said at last.

"Are you serious?" Nuf Ced asked. *'Pit-too.*

Fox reached up and pulled at Casey's sleeve. "You're not serious, are you?"

"Sure, for a price." Casey shrugged. "What're the odds on me?"

"A thousand to one," said Nuf Ced. *'Pit-too.*

"I'll take anything he wants at twenty to one," Sullivan snapped, straightening his jacket, and taking another light from Smiler.

Slowly, intently, Casey reached into his breast pocket and removed the five-hundred-dollar bill, and then he raised it high and waved it. "You're on, John L.," Casey said. "For this."

The whole Third Base gasped.

Casey gave the bill to Nuf Ced. "You hold the stakes, Mr. McGreevey."

Sullivan shrugged and wolfed down the last of the ale. "I've whipped a thousand better men than you, sissy pants," he said, wiping the foam off his mustache.

CATCHING UP
WITH THE
CHAMPION

N uf Ced closed the bar, and the entire assembly traipsed down Columbus Avenue to Walpole Street and the South End Grounds, home of the Beaneaters. Nuf Ced tipped the night watchman a dollar, and they all worked to stake out a makeshift ring between the pitcher's box and first base. It was only a couple weeks till the longest day of the year, and there was a good moon and some city light, which came over the high peaked roof and the fancy spires that made South End as fine a ballpark as there was in the thirty-eight states.

"You sure you wanna go through with this, Casey?" Fox asked, helping him off with his coat and tie. "You said you don't even enjoy fighting."

"I don't. But I'm also of the opinion I can beat him and make my fortune."

"Remember, this is The Great John L. When I had Paddy Ryan fight him down in Mississippi in '82, I thought Paddy was the best ever, and Johnny broke his jaw and ruptured him, and Paddy said the very first time Sullivan hit him it was like a telephone pole went through him."

"Yeah, but that was '82. I seen Sullivan fight last night. He's fat as a hog, and he's drunk a lotta ale tonight. Besides, my girl friend left me, and I'm mean."

Fox shrugged. He'd done his best. "Well, all right then, but be careful at the first. Johnny's a fast starter."

Casey had already headed out to the middle of the ring, but now he turned back and shook his head at Fox. "You stick to your magazine editing, Fox. There's a thousand men fought John L. Sullivan, and every last one of them was careful just because he's The Great John L. And every last one of 'em lost."

Fox stroked his chin. "You know, you may be right," he said.

"Up to scratch," Nuf Ced cried out, and the two fighters stepped forward and faced each other.

"Make him suck eggs, Johnny," Smiler Pippen hollered.

"Knock the spots off him," Rosie yelled (not to be outdone).

The other spectators, forming a human ring apron, stood about in a square, screaming in anticipation. "Just because we ain't using gloves don't mean it's not to be a good, clean fight," Nuf Ced said. *'Pit-too.* "Four rounds. No biting, scratching, gouging, tripping or wrestling." Both men nodded. Nuf Ced traced a line across the grass with his toe. "A knockdown, man don't rise to toe the line by the count of ten, fight's over."

"C'mon, c'mon, everybody knows that," Sullivan growled, and he spit on his hands and cocked his arms, fists up.

Nuf Ced looked to Casey to take the same stance, but he barely moved his hands above his waist. "Are you *ready?*" Nuf Ced asked him, and a bit anxiously.

"If you've got the ten thousand dollars."

"I told you. I got Johnny's marker, and it's good. My word."

"C'mon, c'mon," Sullivan said, and then he belched horrendously loud.

Nuf Ced spit and raised his arm. Sullivan knew what to expect. But Casey had it figured out. He didn't even look at Sullivan, but, instead, kept his eyes on Nuf Ced, and the instant his arm moved, Casey ducked. Good thing. The air was shattered by the force of John L.'s blow.

Casey had kept his hands low, and kept them loose, and so he came up then in one motion, banging his right to The Big Fellow's belly, and then the left, and by the time Casey was raised up, Sullivan was retching and actually holding his stomach with his left hand. So Casey stepped in, and, with all his might, pounded his right to the champion's meaty face, and with that, barely a dozen seconds into the fray, Mighty Casey had hit a home run. The Great John L. buckled and fell to the infield grass.

The crowd came to utter silence, shocked. Blood trickled from the corner of Sullivan's mouth, but he wouldn't dab at it, any more than Casey would grab his own throbbing knuckles. Instead, the two men just glared at each other, as Nuf Ced began to count. ". . . three, four . . ." Finally, Sullivan began to rise, and he was up to toe the line at eight.

He reached his feet like a bull elephant, hoisting himself up, but once he'd lifted his great bulk off the ground and leaned forward, then he owned a forward momentum that a sleeker creature wouldn't possess. Sullivan began to pound the few steps toward Casey, and it would have been easy for Casey to step aside, but he suddenly realized that he was backed up against the crowd—John L.'s crowd. Not only did the loyal partisans block Casey's movement, but one grabbed a belt loop, another took hold of his braces, and yet another tripped him. Casey tried to duck, but, as he'd seen the night before, in Nantasket, for all Sullivan's corpulence he still had some agility, and he readjusted and caught Casey dodging down, flush, with an uppercut.

Casey staggered back, his whole face exploding, his brains rattling about. He couldn't even offer a defense when Sullivan moved in and, with his left, chopped Casey again. He wanted to go down and regroup; he knew it was best to put aside his pride, take the fall and clear his head on the ground. But this time the spectators not only blocked Casey's fall, but they propped him up, and then they bounced him back toward The Big Fellow. Casey was a completely helpless target, and he could see, in his daze, that the champion was winding up for the *coup de grâce*.

But then, incredibly, just like that, Sullivan dropped his dukes and idly watched Casey fly past him, still propelled by the push from the crowd. Sullivan just kept his hands on his hips and glared at the spectators. "Goddamnit, John L. Sullivan doesn't need any help against any man when he's in the ring," he bellowed, and the offenders shrank back, chastened.

Satisfied, then, Sullivan turned to finish off Casey. But the moment was lost; Casey'd had the time to shake his head clear. So, when Sullivan swung, Casey managed to hop aside, as if he were getting away from a high pitch, and with everything left in him, he ducked down and came up throwing, like a shortstop going to first. Whoosh. Into the soft underbelly. Sullivan gagged. His chin was wide open, but Casey went for the tummy again. And again. He could feel his fist burrowing into the paunch as if he were hitting into one of those newfangled air-filled breast protectors that catchers had just started to wear.

Sullivan doubled over, and only then did Casey aim his left hand—the one that still had knuckles intact—for Sullivan's chin. Bam. This time John L. went down fast, herky-jerky. He crumpled to his knees and then pitched forward, spitting out the evening's excess, spilling his beans. Casey stood above him, fists quivering, cocked.

"Start the count, Nuf Ced," Fox screamed. "Start it."

Sullivan peeked up. He didn't know that Casey's hands hurt so much he surely couldn't have risked landing another blow. ". . . three, four . . ." So, John L. ruminated on his circumstance for another beat or so—". . . five, six . . ."—and then sank back onto the infield grass, into his own blood and guts.

". . . nine, ten!" cried out Nuf Ced, and The Great John L. was beaten.

Fox rushed to Casey and raised his hand, which shot up in eerie silence, for the crowd itself was dead quiet. Finally, in fact, it was Sullivan, wiping the mess from his face, who spoke up. "Congratulations, sonny," he said. "Now you can tell the whole world you was the first sonuvab— You was the first man ever to lick The Great John L."

"Tell? Gimme my ten thousand dollars, and I'll never whisper it to a soul on God's green earth," Casey said. "I just wanna marry my girl."

"Don't matter none what you say," Sullivan pouted. "That viper Fox'll put it in the *Gazette*."

Fox left Casey and walked over to where Sullivan lay. He put his hands on his hips and looked down. "Not if you fight Kilrain, I won't, Johnny."

Sullivan raised himself up on an elbow and scratched his head. "Yeah now?" he said, and then he looked all around at the crowd. "Any sonuvabitch here see John L. Sullivan get beat tonight?"

There was silence for another moment, as the spectators all looked at one another. Finally, it was Nuf Ced: *'Pit-too,* he went, and then: "No indeed, not me," in a loud, clear voice.

And after that they all cried out: "Not these eyes!" "No, no indeed." "Why, I didn't see nuthin'." "Never in my sight!"

Sullivan nodded. "All right, Fox, I'll fight your boy."

"Bare-knuckle, Johnny."

"Yeah, yeah, yeah. Bare-knuckle. One last time." And The Big Fellow shook his head with resignation and put out his hand to Casey. "Well, congratulations, Mister," Sullivan said. "If I had to get beat, I'm glad it was to an American."

Casey nodded, dusted himself off, picked up his jacket and shirt and tie, and started to walk away. "Get me my money, Fox" was all he called out, and then he turned to the crowd. Suddenly, magically, a swath was cut for him. The people pushed back, jamming into each other, eyeing him with awe, afraid even to whisper, let alone to get in the way of the first man who beat John L. Sullivan, The Boston Strong Boy.

As soon as Casey had gotten through the crowd, the path closed back up, so when Fox took after Casey, he had to fight his way, and he didn't catch up with him till Casey was well back of home plate. Fox reached up, then, and took his diamond-studded gold horseshoe pin off, and pinned it on Casey's shirt. "Thanks" was all Fox said.

Casey looked down at the pin, and then he took it off. "You never worked a circus, did you, Fox?" he asked.

"No."

Casey put the pin back on his shirt, but this time he affixed it with the open end up. "You never hang a horseshoe down. Anybody on a circus knows that. Hang it down, all the luck will run out the ends." Fox nodded. "No wonder you never beat John L. before," Casey said.

13

CASEY AT THE BAT

Flossie was hanging out the wash on the clothesline the next afternoon when Casey came tearing up to her. He already had been to his boardinghouse and changed into his uniform, but all Flossie saw was the mouse under his eye, the mark on his chin. "Timothy, what in heaven's—"

"I haven't got time to explain," he said. "I'm already late for the game, and I've gotta see Drinkwater, too."

Flossie gritted her teeth at the mere mention of that man's name, but Casey only reached out and, before she understood what he was doing, pinned the horseshoe pin above her breast. "We can pluck the diamonds out and make a proper engagement ring," he said, and, with that, he dashed off to the ballyard.

Flossie was flabbergasted. She had to unfasten the pin and take it off to see clearly. And that only turned her curiosity more to anger. Why, this pin obviously cost even more than the silk dress. How much more money was Drinkwater paying him now to perform his dirty deeds? Furious, Flossie pinned the horseshoe back on, and even though barely half the wash had gone up, she left the balance right there in the basket and rushed off to the Grounds.

There had never been a larger crowd for a baseball game in Mudville. Had everybody in town skipped work? Had every boy robbed his piggy bank? Why, there must have been five thousand in attendance after grumpy old Cyrus Weatherly stuck the overflow behind ropes in center field. Ernest Thayer had arrived on the Worcester train in time to get a ticket, but the crowd spilled over into the aisles, and he had a hard time seeing some of the action.

But where was Casey? Mighty Casey? Nobody knew.

At last, Willie Flaherty, the Mudville manager, had sent someone over to check for Casey at his boardinghouse, but, of course, he wasn't there. When the umpire took the field and asked for the lineups, Casey was just then boarding the first Saturday train to Mudville. But who knew? There wasn't yet telephone service from Boston to Mudville, and what was Casey to do, send a telegram that said: SORRY STOP DELAYED IN BOSTON IN FIGHT STOP SEE YOU SOON? No. And when he wasn't announced in the starting nine, it caused such a commotion in the stands that before the game could begin, the announcer had to pick up his megaphone and go back out on the field and explain that Casey was . . . well, lost. The announcement was met with gasps; the cranks didn't know whether to boo or cry or scream.

Only Drinkwater, sitting in his box by the Mudville bench, beamed. Still, he scratched his chin. The kid wasn't supposed to take a powder *yet*. First he was supposed to screw up for a few games, act like he'd suddenly lost his ginger—then disappear. But to fail to show up before a great throng like this—well, Drinkwater thought, maybe that was even more dramatic, more painful for these faithful rubes.

Willie Flaherty kept the same Mudville lineup, only inserting his best reserve, Lawrence "Ears" McGillicuddy, in Casey's third spot in the batting order, behind Johnny Flynn, leading off, and Jimmy Blake. Anyway, Mudville had their best wheelman, Barry O'Connor, in the pitcher's box, so maybe they wouldn't even need Mighty Casey. But it was not so. Without their star, the home nine was at sea. They never once even managed a rally. Mudville did get two runs in the fourth, but that was only because the young Lynn pitcher momentarily lost his control, and then the center fielder, backed up against the overflow crowd, muffed what should have been an easy fly ball for the third out.

Meanwhile, the Lynns scored three in the top of the first, when the crowd and players alike were still buzzing about where Casey might be, and then they added a single run in the fourth when the cleanup man doubled, and then the next batter stitched a single to right, and McGillicuddy threw wild. Drinkwater curled his mustache, happily, and chortled to himself as the crowd booed.

It was still 4–2 for the Lynns in the top of the seventh, two down, nobody on, when here came Casey into the Grounds. The place exploded, the roars lifting out of the stadium and carrying above all the rooftops of Mudville. Casey was back! Mighty Casey! The Mudville nine was saved!

Drinkwater gleefully fingered his gold watch chain, and winked at Casey as he ran to the bench. This kid has an even better sense of theater than I could have imagined, he mused. To show up like this and *then* strike out—an even greater disappointment for the gullible locals.

The Lynn batter grounded out to short for the third out, and Casey hopped over to Flaherty. "I'm ready to swing the ash, Willie," he said.

In the stands, by first base, a burly gentleman in a waist-coat rose. "Sit downnn," hollered a fellow with a cigar, behind him.

"Naww," said the crank on his feet. "I was out here a couple weeks ago when we played Brockton, and at the start of the seventh a pretty young lady stood up to stretch and Casey espied her and promptly larruped the sphere over the left-field wall. He'll be up now in this seventh, and no telling what he'll do at the bat if we all rise." And he beckoned to the crowd, and those around him began to get to their feet, and then the others farther away, and soon Drinkwater in his box and Ernest Thayer, down the third-base line, were lifted up

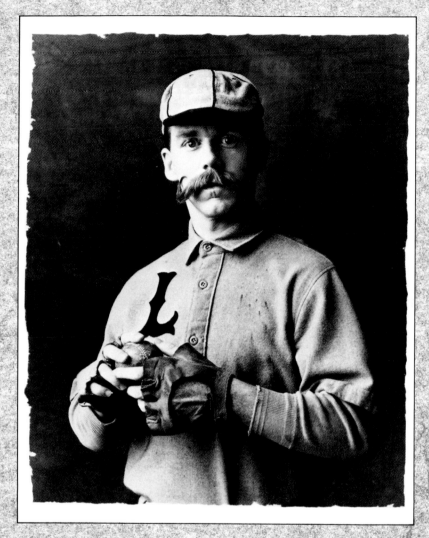

Said Landis,
"It was the best pitch
I ever threw"

in this human wave, and now the whole five thousand were on their feet.

But Willie Flaherty wasn't looking at the crowd. He only stared back at Casey. "I play the gentlemen who are here when the game starts," he snapped.

"Listen, Willie, I can explain," Casey said, but the manager merely folded his arms and spit.

"Come on, Jimmy, start it off," he called out to Blake, who was striding toward the plate. "McGillicuddy—come on, Ears, get on deck!"

Casey lowered his head and sank down onto the bench. The crowd took its seats. Blake popped to second, and when poor McGillicuddy came to the plate then, they booed him and screamed to Flaherty: "Come on, put Casey in!" But the manager just crossed his legs and spit, and McGillicuddy, rattled, managed only to bump a little dribbler back to the wheelman. And then Yesterday Phillips struck out; three up and three down. "A fat lot of good that stretching before the seventh inning did," the loudmouth with the cigar hooted at the burly gentleman in the waistcoat.

"Well now, we'll give it another try sometime," he replied.

The eighth was no better for Mudville, which was especially bad because Barry O'Connor, in the pitcher's box, was only getting stronger. Both sides failed to get a man on, but when Mudville batted, Flaherty didn't even glance over in Casey's direction.

A handful of cranks left then, and Flossie, who had found her way in by the bleacher gate, was able to move closer and peek at some of the action when she moved this way and that. When the Mudvilles took the field for the top of the ninth, Flossie had only a few spectators in front of her, and she could behold Casey, still sitting glumly on the bench.

O'Connor got through the ninth without incident, and then he and old Jimmy Blake, the shortstop, moved together intently toward Flaherty. "Come on, Willie," O'Connor said, "whatever Casey's done, don't go punishing the whole team."

"It's not like you never been in a whiskey hole yourself," Blake added.

Flaherty glanced over toward Casey and spit. "All right, tell you what," he said. "If we get to McGillicuddy's spot, I'll bat Casey for Ears."

Blake and O'Connor raised a happy cry and let the other players in on the good news. But this elation on the bench was short-lived because Cooney fouled out to the catcher on the very first pitch, and Barrows grounded out weakly to first. "I've never seen such a sickly silence," Ernest Thayer said to the fellow next to him.

"A straggling few are even leaving in deep despair," the other gentleman said. "Still, I'd put up even money if Casey could get at the bat."

The pitcher for the Lynn nine was a wiry little lad named Kenny Landis, who was, in fact, a law student pitching under the *nom de baseball* of Walt Mueller. In his heavy flannel, Landis/Mueller was sweating copiously as he peered in for the final out of the game against Johnny Flynn. Landis shook his head. Home plate was only twelve inches across then (as opposed to the seventeen inches it's been all this century), and now, to Landis, it didn't look any bigger than a horseshoe. He perspired all the more, and tried to dry his pitching hand on his trousers, but they were almost soaked clear through with sweat.

"Come on, Johnny, fall into it," Casey called out from the bench, fingering his favorite bat, a black Spalding Old Wagon Tongue model.

Landis was truly tired, too. He hung an inshoot, and Flynn knocked it cleanly up the middle. The crowd was suddenly prepared to believe now, and Flossie's heart fluttered. Jimmy Blake stepped into the batsman's box, but when the Grounds exploded, even Blake knew that the roar wasn't for him. No, the cheers were for what might come after Blake: Casey, Mighty Casey, was moving up on deck.

Casey had picked up another Spalding, and he swung the two bats as he came off the bench. But he didn't go directly to the on-deck spot. No, instead he detoured over to the front-row boxes, toward where Chester Drinkwater sat.

Out in center field, behind the rope, a lanky farmer who'd come all the way down from Nashua, New Hampsire, to see Casey play, let Flossie slide in front of him, so she was now in the front row, right smack in the middle of the overflow. Flossie could clearly see Casey consorting with Drinkwater again. And right out in the open! Right here before God and all of Mudville! Flossie slammed her arms folded across her chest and cursed the best way she knew how, which wasn't much at all, really, so then she cursed the way she knew others did better. "Damn you, Timothy F. X. Casey," she said, "damn your hide."

Casey left Drinkwater and came on deck, calling encouragement out to Blake. Jimmy was an old-timer, cagey when he was sober, and he could see that Casey's mere appearance had rattled the kid pitcher, so he decided to rip into the first pitch. Good idea. Landis had aimed it, and it was fat, and Blake rifled it down the line. When the dust had lifted, he was standing on second and Flynn on third.

And here came Casey. And here came the cheers, rising to the heavens. By now, too, poor Landis could barely see through his sweat. Casey was no dummy; he made him sweat some more. He took the time to briefly take off his cap, acknowledge the cheers, and he took even more time to rub some dirt into his hands and wipe them across his shirtfront.

Landis tried to compose himself. He decided that Casey would probably want to see what kind of stuff a strange new pitcher had, so he'd be taking. Lawyers tended to be bright in those days, and Landis had the mind to match his moxie. He laid in a waist-high fastball, and Casey let it go by. "Strike one," the umpire said.

Behind the center-field rope, Flossie bowed her head and wrenched her hands and prayed that Casey would find his conscience again and lay into the ball.

Landis had gained some confidence, so now, rather than throw another fastball, he decided to come in with an offshoot at a different speed. It was close, but the umpire, standing well back of the catcher, saw the pitch nick the inside corner. "Strike two," he said, and the crowd booed.

Still, Casey wasn't worried. He even nodded to calm the cranks down, and then he stepped out of the batsman's box and stared at Landis. Casey had seen the lad's repertoire now, and it wasn't anything he couldn't deal with. Besides, Casey owned a feared reputation as a good two-strike hitter. The crowd was on its feet, hollering, as Casey stepped back into the batsman's box, and even on tiptoes, Ernest Thayer had to dodge this way and that to see clearly.

In fact, Thayer missed it at that moment when Casey, focusing on the pitcher, suddenly saw Flossie, directly behind, watching him from straightaway center. She stood out clearly against the crowd in her maid's uniform. For just a moment then, Casey smiled at her, and something came over him, and before he knew what he'd done, he'd raised his bat and was pointing it toward center, signaling that he would hit a home run right over his dear Flossie's head. The crowd roared again, all the more, all the more astonished. "What was that? What was that?" Thayer cried out.

"I couldn't see it either," the guy next to him said. But just then the crowd parted some, and Thayer was clearly able to see Casey clench his teeth and pound Old Wagon Tongue on home plate. Landis sweated even more. He would have wanted to go to the resin bag, only there weren't any resin bags yet, so he rubbed his hands on his clothes, on his cap, his socks, his hair, his mustache.

And then, at last, he was ready, his right foot on the rear line of the box, and he held the ball before him, and took the step he was allowed and let the pitch fly.

Casey saw the ball all the way. The pitch didn't have a thing on it. It loomed as big as the moon hanging over Nantasket Beach. So Casey began his swing, poised, evenly, perfectly, and . . .

Casey missed it by a country mile.

14

MUDVILLE'S SOUR REACTION

M udville blinked. Mudville couldn't believe it. Flossie could. Flossie cried. Casey had gone on the take. Casey had struck out. There was no joy in Mudville.

15

AN ELECTRIFYING TURN OF EVENTS

Only . . . wait.

The pitch that Landis threw had darted down as it went across the plate, and now it passed under the catcher's glove. It began to roll to the backstop. Shocked, Casey still just stood there in the batsman's box. He was as frozen as Fairfax and Siegfried, human statues. "Run, Casey, run" came the cries, and his ears pricked up, and here came Johnny Flynn, already bearing down on the plate.

Finally, Casey came to life and began to run for first. The catcher got to the ball, picked it up, dropped it, picked it up again, and there went the throw, soaring over the first base-man's head by a good five feet. Flynn scored. It was 4–3. And here came old Jimmy Blake, chugging right behind. Tie score. Four-up.

By now Casey was on his way to second. He rounded the bag, so when the rightfielder picked up the horsehide, he threw behind Casey, to try and nail him as he sought to scramble back to second. Only Casey saw where the throw was going, and he didn't so much as pause. Instead, he put his head down and churned toward third. The second sacker took the throw—it was a good one—and he whirled and whipped the ball to third.

The Mudville third-base coach, Mike Gallagher, screamed at Casey. "Slide, Casey, slide!" he hollered, and Casey did, just as the relay from second came in, low. It skidded in the dirt, and then it ricocheted off the third base-man's shoulder and bounced a ways down the leftfield line. "Head for home, Casey!" the coacher screamed, and Casey scrambled to his feet and was on his way, lickety-split.

The third sacker tore back, picked up the ball, and fired it to the plate. Casey slid. The catcher took the throw neat and slapped the ball on him. "Safe!" the umpire said.

"Curses," Chester Drinkwater muttered.

There was joy in Mudville. Mudville 5–Lynn 4. The cranks banged one another on the backs, tossed their hats in the June air, and, here and there, the most decorous of women allowed themselves to be publicly bussed by men they barely knew. It was bedlam. Casey himself thought how unbeliev-able it was that Princess Clara, with the aid of her amazing electric belt, had called the future right on the button. But he couldn't even move off home plate. First his teammates had descended upon him, and then the crowd poured onto the field, and as soon as the men of Mudville reached Casey, they hoisted him to their shoulders. He had struck out, but the team had won, so they lifted him high, cheered his name, and began to parade him about.

The mob had carried Casey all the way out to second base when he spotted Flossie. She was all by herself, still standing where she'd watched him strike out. The rest of the center-field crowd had dashed in to join the celebration, so there stood Flossie, alone, the tears flowing down her rosy-red cheeks. "Let me down!" Casey cried out. "Let me down!" And when the happy people wouldn't, he fought his way off their shoulders to the ground, scrambling away from the cranks who kept calling his great name and pounding his broad back. Then he ran to Flossie, ran as fast as he could, ran even faster than he had just circled the bases.

Only when he got to Flossie and grabbed her, this is what she said to him, word for word: "I hate you, Timothy Casey. I hate you."

"Listen to me, Flossie." And Casey even shook her some. "Damnit! Listen to me. I tried at the bat. I did. I tried! *I tried!*" Casey slumped. "He just struck me out."

"Well, I don't believe you a'tall," Flossie said, and she twisted away from him.

"But you must," Casey screamed. "It happens. Sooner or later. Listen, somewhere someday somebody's even . . . even . . . even gonna beat John L. Sullivan."

But Flossie didn't have the time for any foolish analogies. "You cheated us all!" she cried, and she walked away from Casey and jammed her hands to her hips.

He was going to hurry over after her, but at that moment Casey felt a tap on his shoulder. All around him, the Lynn players were filing out, and when Casey looked back, there was Landis, the kid pitcher. He was the one who had tapped Casey. "Mr. Casey," he said, "no matter what happened, I just want you to know it was an honor facing you. And I want you to know that even if you won, that last pitch was the best one I ever hurled in all my life. I don't even know how I did it."

"It was sure some pitch," Casey said, patting the boy on his pitching arm. "If you can throw that pitch again, you can strike out King Kelly hisself."

"You can be sure I'm gonna keep trying," Landis said.

Only he never was able to throw that pitch again. He tried. Oh, how he tried. He tried holding the ball this way and that, stepping in such a manner, releasing the horsehide here and there, firing it fast and slow. But all Landis did was give himself a sore arm and hurry himself into the judiciary. That was because Landis didn't realize that he'd mixed his sweat with his mustache wax and thereby thrown the first spitball in history, but since Landis didn't know that, he could never do it again, and nobody invented the spitball for real for another fourteen years.

Casey jabbed Landis in the chest, and then he grabbed him and yanked him over to Flossie. "Listen to this," he said to her, and then he whirled on Landis. "Tell her, tell her what you told me," he screamed at the poor fellow.

"Well, ma'm, like I told Mr. Casey, no matter what happened, it was just a real honor being able to pitch against—"

"No, no," Casey screamed. "Not that."

"What?" said Landis.

"Yeah, what?" said Flossie. None of this was impressing her even a little bit.

"The part about the pitch."

"The last pitch?"

"Of course: the last pitch."

"Well," said Landis, "as I was saying—"

"Stop saying and say it."

"Well, it—"

Casey turned Landis toward Flossie. "Tell her. You already told me."

"Well, ma'm, it was far and away the best pitch I ever threw. Ever. To anybody."

Casey grabbed Landis's hand and pumped it. "You hear that, Flossie? He just plain struck me out. He was just better'n me."

But Flossie wasn't altogether convinced and moved away from Casey. He chased after her. Landis just stood there, watching. Some of his teammates from the Lynn nine also stopped and watched Casey carrying on. Pottsy Callahan, the catcher, even threw his glove and mask and breast protector down and took a seat right there on the outfield grass to watch the proceedings.

"Well, I don't believe you," Flossie said.

"You've got to," Casey said.

Pottsy Callahan called out: "Lady, it wasn't just the best pitch this kid threw. It was the best pitch I ever seen any wheelman toss."

"You see?" Casey said.

At least Flossie turned back to Casey. "I don't care what all these players say. I can't believe *you*. Why, I even saw you talking to Drinkwater before you went to the bat."

Casey started to respond, then he saw all the Lynn players and some cranks were listening, intently waiting to hear what he had to say, so he took Flossie by the arm and steered her away from the bystanders. "That was because I told Drinkwater I left his five hundred dollars and the silk dress with Phoebe at the Parker House, because you were right, and I don't want nothing to do with his deal."

Flossie looked curiously at Casey now, puzzled, unsure. He took her by the cheeks and held her face before him. "Don't you hear me, Flossie? I love you! I *love* you!"

He screamed this so loudly that, in fact, everybody heard Casey, and Pottsy Callahan and Kenny Landis and some of the other Lynn ballists applauded. And then some of the cranks started cheering. Casey held up his hand to stop the applause and looked back at Flossie. Unfortunately, she appeared to still be considering this, so Casey pulled out all the stops. He sank to one knee, took her sweet hands in his, and said: "Florence Cleary, will you do me the honor of being my wife?"

Flossie believed him. "Yes, I will," she said.

Casey jumped to his feet and took her in his arms and kissed her, and all the players and the cranks who were standing around watching cheered one last time, loudest of all, and then they went on their way, leaving Flossie and Casey alone together in center field.

Casey said: "It's a good thing for you, you said that, because I'm also a rich man now. I got ten one-thousand-dollar bills in my shoes."

"What?"

"I'll tell you all about it sometime, but right now—" and Casey reached over and took off the horseshoe pin, because he had just noticed that Flossie had it on upside down. "Don't ever wear a horseshoe pin pointing down, because then all the luck will run out of it," he said, and he pinned it back on her, the right way.

Then he put his arm around her, and they walked off together, toward the sunset, as a matter of fact. But Flossie scrunched up her face a little bit. She said, "You mean, if I'd worn the pin right you'd have hit a home run over my head, the way you pointed?"

"Nah," Casey said, "nobody coulda hit that pitch. You gotta understand, darling: in baseball, even the best ballists only get a hit one out of every three times up."

We can make it ~~as easy~~ special

"We can make it
a proper engagement ring,"
said Casey

AN EPILOGUE

◆

IN WHICH THE READER IS
PERMITTED TO ASCERTAIN
WHAT BEFELL VARIOUS OF THE PRINCIPALS
SUBSEQUENT TO SATURDAY,
JUNE 2ND, 1888 . . .

John L. Sullivan kept his word to Richard Fox and fought Jake Kilrain the next July 9, defending his title in seventy-five rounds, the last bare-knuckle title bout ever fought. The next time Sullivan stepped into the prize ring, three years later, he had gloves on, and Gentleman Jim Corbett took the heavyweight crown from Sullivan by knocking him out in the twenty-first round. "My friends, I have fought once too often," Sullivan announced. "But, if I had to get licked, I'm glad it was by an American!"

Sullivan's profligate ways cost him increasingly, though, and soon he was bankrupt, popping out the diamonds from his championship belt to pay for drinks and other indulgences. His legend never waned, though, and when he died, age fifty-nine, in 1918, the news made banner headlines across the forty-eight states.

◆

Richard Fox remained one of the pillars of popular American journalism, and under his stewardship *The National Police Gazette* continued to prosper for many more years, offering an editorial mix of sex, sport and crime that serves the multitudes well to this very day, especially if you add weather.

◆

Jim Naismith invented basketball in 1891.

◆

Nuf Ced McGreevey continued to preside over his sports saloon until Prohibition. To this day no Boston baseball team has ever won the world championship without Nuf Ced being present at all home games. This places a considerable obstacle in the path of current Red Sox clubs, inasmuch as Mr. McGreevey has not visited Fenway Park in the last half-century, since the occasion of his death.

◆

Phoebe Alexander and Smiler Pippen made each other's acquaintance one night early in 1893 at the Third Base Saloon. They were well met, married later that year and soon thereafter found religion.

As stalwart members of the Lord's Day Alliance, they

worked diligently for the rest of their lives to keep the Sabbath holy, undefiled by those twin temptations, baseball games and trolley cars.

◆

Meanwhile, Chester Drinkwater, The *World's* Trolley King, became recognized as one of the half-dozen richest men in America by the turn of the century. The bulk of his fortune was gained by building ballyards and amusement parks outside cities, and then running streetcar lines to them, selling real estate along the way—plots of land that were filled largely with little white houses with picket fences running around them.

The only locale where this scheme didn't work was Mudville, where, at considerable loss, Drinkwater let many land options lapse in 1889.

Returning from his honeymoon on the *Titanic* with his fourth wife, the Countess Nina von Munschauer, twenty-three, Drinkwater went to a watery grave at the age of sixty-four.

◆

Grumpy old Cyrus Weatherly, the town miser, refurbished Mudville Grounds after the profitable '88 season, so that for decades after it was called Weatherly Park, though it was known everywhere as "the jewel of the bushes."

Taking this cue, Alfred L. Evans Jr., second vice-president of The First Farmers and Mechanics Bank of Mudville, proposed that his institution support the redevelopment of the entire East Side. This venture proved so successful that when the president of FF&M retired, Mr. Evans was jumped over the first vice-president and made bank president. The area itself became an early national model for downtown renewal.

Only after World War I, when the East Side had turned largely Italian, Lithuanian and Pole, was the old Mudville Grounds razed, to be replaced by a regional high school. East High was the center of the community for many years, but in the 1950s, as the younger residents of the area began to move to the new suburbs, the school was torn down, the school district consolidated, and a real estate developer put in middle-class housing for blacks. The area is now known as Covent Gardens Estates, and on the actual site of the diamond where Casey struck out, there is a twenty-four-hour convenience store.

◆

Timothy F. X. Casey finished the '88 season with Mudville, but although he continued to have a fine year, the events of those days in late May and early June seemed to extract some spirit from him that he never rediscovered on the diamond. Besides, he grew all the more in love with Flossie, and they became engaged. As Casey had suggested, they took Richard Fox's horseshoe pin, pulled out a couple of the diamonds and made an engagement ring. Then, on the day after the season ended, late in September, they eloped. They alighted from the train in Springfield, took separate rooms in the old Springfield Grand Hotel and sought out a priest the next morning.

However, upon learning of Casey's disreputable profession—a ballist!—none of the local clergy would perform the wedding ceremony. Flossie then recalled Jim Naismith's visit, they contacted him at the YMCA college, and Naismith gladly spoke up for the two young lovers. So it was that Monsignor Terrence FitzGerald joined them in Holy Matrimony on Tuesday, October 2nd, 1888.

Casey and Flossie took their wedding night in Springfield, and the next day Casey graciously consented to instruct Naismith's students in the proper mechanics of hitting a baseball. During the class, Flossie went out and purchased a large valise. When she and Casey left Mudville so hastily, they had discovered that they needed another bag, but they didn't have time to get one then, so they had just thrown their extra belongings into a couple of peach baskets that Flossie found in the Evanses' pantry.

These were left behind at the college gymnasium when the Caseys departed Springfield, and were, evidently, forgotten until that fateful day in 1891 when Naismith designed basketball. "They must've been the Caseys'," Naismith said many years later, when he was residing in Lawrence, Kansas, as the coach of the University of Kansas basketball team. "Why else would there have been peach baskets lying around a gymnasium?" A good thing, too. If Casey had not brought the peach baskets to Springfield, it is likely that basketball players would still be shooting at a square target.

Flossie and Timothy Casey spent the next couple of years traveling America, investing their fortune in prime real estate, purchasing downtown tracts in such humble minor-league towns as Dallas, Texas; Seattle, Washington; and Los Angeles, California. However, all this time Casey had never stopped thinking about what Mr. Evans had mentioned to him once back in Mudville, and so, when Flossie became pregnant, he went back to school, enrolling, in the autumn of 1891, in the very first freshman class at a small new institution in Palo Alto, California, that was known as Leland Stanford Jr. University. He graduated, with high honors, in 1895.

The Caseys then settled nearby, in the town of Stockton, where he quickly made his mark in trolleys. Flossie bore him four daughters, and Casey became a pillar of the community—daily communicant, councilman and, finally, philanthropist.

Thayer's poem became more and more famous, inspiring vaudeville skits, books, paintings, songs, movies, additional poems, even a whole opera. As common and vulgar as the subject matter may be, the work is widely considered to be the most classic comic American poem. Thayer never wrote another word in his life that anyone recalls, while generations of schoolchildren grew up able to recite all 577 words of "Casey at the Bat, A Ballad of the Republic," verbatim.

A noted vaudevillian, DeWolf Hopper, made the poem his signature, reciting it, all told, on more than ten thousand occasions. Once Hopper even appeared at the Stockton Opera House, and Mr. and Mrs. Casey took the four girls to see the performance. Casey leaned over to Flossie and whispered that he thought Hopper had given a fine recital.

Flossie agreed, but she also wondered why Thayer had

ended the poem where he did and not gone on with the whole story. "Oh, you know sportswriters," Casey whispered. "They always only tell it their way." And he shrugged and went back to watching the next act, which was Wilbur Willow, Ventriloquist, with his little friend, Benjie.

Casey patted Flossie's hand. "Reminds me of Nantasket Beach," he said.

"Oh no, nothing could ever be so fine," Flossie replied. "Ever."

"Shhh," said Joan, the oldest daughter.

"Be quiet, Mother," said Mary Louise, the next oldest. All four of the girls liked the ventriloquist more than they did DeWolf Hopper.

Casey smiled and patted Flossie's hand again. He could feel her engagement ring. It had new stones in it. Long ago she had put the original diamonds back into the horseshoe pin. She didn't have the horseshoe pin on this night, at the vaudeville show. She wore it only for very special occasions.

Neither Casey nor Flossie ever told their girls that their father was the true hero of Ernest Thayer's poem. This was somewhat ironic, because, in a way, "Casey" became the American Dauphin, as, for years, all sorts of washed-up old ballplayers went around maintaining that they had been the model for the Mighty Casey.

But, in fact, in all his life, Casey told only one person that he was the Casey of the poem. That was his nephew George, son of Casey's left-handed twin sister, Kate. Once, in 1909, when he had to travel East on trolley business, Casey visited Kate in Baltimore, and the young lad seemed so completely keen on baseball that Casey took him over to a corner table there in the family saloon on Conway Street and told him all about the old days of baseball and especially the tale of '88.

Young George was particularly enthralled with the part about Casey pointing to center field, daring to foretell a home run. "Imagine a player havin' the nerve to do a thing like that," George said.

"Well"—Casey chuckled—"if any other batsman ever pulls that fool stunt again, I strongly advise him to make sure then he really *does* hit a home run."

After Casey retired from the trolley business, he played a lot of golf. He was long off the tee but dicey around the greens. He and Flossie traveled a great deal. Once they made the Grand Tour of Europe, and they also went to such places as Honolulu, Lake Louise and the 1932 Olympic Games in Los Angeles. They had an even dozen grandchildren, but, of course, the name Casey had run out.

Then, in the spring of 1941, Casey's health began to fail, and he took to his bed in June. He knew the jig was up. He just got weaker and weaker. It was the seventy-fifth summer of his good life.

Three of his daughters still lived in and around Stockton, but Mary Louise had moved to San Francisco, so Flossie called her and said she'd better come quickly. Mary Louise brought with her her youngest son, Casey's favorite grandchild, the one he had named John Lawrence Sullivan Gambardella. They just made it to Stockton, to the old family house, in time; it was the evening of July 17th. Mary Louise and John went directly to the master bedroom, where the old man lay.

"Well, Johnny, how's tricks?" Casey said, barely managing to get the words out. He was going fast now. Peacefully, but fast, the sands of his time, 1867–1941.

"Oh, I'm okay, Grandpop," the boy said, "but I just heard on the radio: the Indians got DiMaggio out tonight. So his streak ends at fifty-six in a row."

Casey shook his head just a little bit. "Well," he said, "if the boy's any good, he'll get over it."

"Yes sir."

Mary Louise kissed her father, and then she stepped back by her sisters so that her mother could stand closest to the old man. Flossie leaned down and kissed Casey gently on the forehead and squeezed his hand. He saw the horseshoe pin on her dress, and then he sighed and his eyes began to close. By now, everyone in the room could all but see the angels who had come to fetch him home.

But then, somehow, Casey forced one more breath of life into his body, and he opened his eyes, even smiled a tiny little bit, and reached up, with all that was left in him, and touched the horseshoe pin. Then his hand fell back down, but his eyes stayed on his beloved Flossie, and this is what he said: "Oh, somewhere in this favored land the sun is shining bright."

And with that, Casey closed off his smile, turned down his eyes and died. Flossie took hold of his hand and said: "The band is playing somewhere, and somewhere hearts are light."

She did not miss a beat. The four daughters turned to look

at one another, tears in their eyes, but wondering what in the world had come over their mother. "And somewhere men are laughing," Flossie went on, "and somewhere children shout."

She smiled broadly and did not say another word.

◆

As for the one other principal in the story, as for baseball, it grew to become the national pastime and lived happily ever after.

THE END

. . . It is very questionable whether there is any public sport in the civilized portion of the world so eminently fitted for the people it was made for as the American national game of base ball. In every respect it is an outdoor sport admirably adapted for our mercurial population. It is full of excitement, is quickly played, and it not only requires vigor of constitution and a healthy physique, but manly courage, steady nerve [and] plenty of pluck.

—Introduction,
*Spalding's Official
Base Ball Guide,*
1888

THE AUTHOR WISHES
TO EXPRESS A SPECIAL DEBT
OF GRATITUDE
TO
ERNEST L. THAYER